FIVE REASONS WHY YOU'LL LOVE THIS BOOK . . .

wi
na
ut

to school!

Hello!

I love being a writer—and one of the most exciting things about telling stories is that you can do it in so many different ways! When I was young, I enjoyed the Asterix and Tintin books, and also weekly comics, which I read from cover to cover.

I've always wanted to have a go at writing a story in comic strip—and so I'm RIDICULOUSLY excited about ELECTRIGIRL which is illustrated by my amazing buddy Cathy Brett. We've had such fun developing Holly's story in words AND pictures! You can see, just by flicking through the book, how we swap from one to the other.

If you've thought about reading comics but weren't sure where to start, try the awesome Phoenix Comic, which comes out weekly and is STUFFED full of brilliant and bonkers comic stories. Or if superheroes are your thing, you can watch videos and play games online at **marvelkids.disney.co.uk** and even design your own comic!

Happy reading!

CHARACTER PROFILES

HOLLY loves sports but hates being the centre of attention, which is a bit of a drawback when you have superpowers!

JOE is obsessed with comics. He's Holly's brother and her mentor, seeing as he knows so much about superheroes.

IMOGEN never goes anywhere without a sketchbook. Resourceful and clever, she has a great imagination.

PROFESSOR MACAVITY is a technological genius bent on world domination – but she's reckoned without Electrigirl and her friends!

FOR JEMIMA AND HARRIET
—MY OWN SUPERHEROES
J. C.

FOR MY SUPERHERO NIECE DAISY,
WITH LOVE
C. B.

OXFORD
UNIVERSITY PRESS

Great Clarendon Street, Oxford OX2 6DP
Oxford University Press is a department of the University of Oxford.
It furthers the University's objective of excellence in research, scholarship,
and education by publishing worldwide. Oxford is a registered trade mark
of Oxford University Press in the UK and in certain other countries

First published 2016

British Library Cataloguing in Publication Data

Data available

ISBN: 978-0-19-274355-8

3 5 7 9 10 8 6 4 2

Printed in Great Britain

Paper used in the production of this book is a natural,
recyclable product made from wood grown in sustainable forests.
The manufacturing process conforms to the environmental
regulations of the country of origin.

ELECTRIGIRL

JO COTTERILL
ILLUSTRATED BY CATHY BRETT

OXFORD
UNIVERSITY PRESS

HOW IT ALL BEGAN

If I hadn't argued with my best friend, I'd never have been struck by lightning. But if I hadn't been struck by lightning, I'd never have got my SUPERPOWERS.

Maybe sometimes, things happen for a reason.

That day, I was on the hilltop, high above the sea. It's the place I always go when I want to be alone. The air was still and strangely hot. Clouds clashed and rolled and rumbled above me, like the thoughts thudding and crashing in my head. How did everything get so awful?

A yellowish tinge to the sky made everything look wrong. The grass was the wrong shade of green; the sea was the wrong shade of blue. My fingers tingled, and the back of my neck prickled, like all the hairs were standing on end.

I re-played the argument over and over in my head: 'How could you?' I'd yelled. 'How could you let me down?'

And she'd just walked away.

What had happened to her? Even her smile was wrong these days.

Everything was wrong.

A faint CRACKLING noise came from behind me. I turned and looked up at the huge new mobile phone mast on the very peak of the hill. Sparks fizzed around the grey globe at its top, like one of those plasma balls. I hesitated. A storm was coming—a big one. And if there was going to be lightning, then I probably shouldn't be up here next to a big metal tower.

I glanced back at the sea, and caught my breath. A light had appeared on the horizon. The sun peeping through? No, it was too small and too bright and too sudden.

It was getting bigger.

Closer.

Brighter.

What was it? Should I move? But where would I run to?

Maybe it was a meteor! A flaming ball of rock

headed straight for me! Was I about to die?

Regret rushed through me: I should have tried harder to keep my friend; I should have told my family I loved them; I should have admitted it was me who dropped Mum's toothbrush in the toilet . . .

AND NOW . . .
NOW IT WAS TOO LATE
FOR ALL OF THAT!

CHAPTER 1

I'm getting ahead of myself. Let me take you back a month. Back to where all of this started, really, with the opening of the new ⊛**CyberSky** building in town.

CyberSky is a mobile phone company. We have a TERRIBLE signal down here on the coast and half the time we end up on a French network, which costs silly money. CyberSky said we'd all get five bars from now on, so I was kind of pleased that they were here. But Bluehaven is *full* of people who get upset and **shout** about the tiniest things, so it had been all over the news before the building was even finished. Yup, you've guessed it, not much happens here.

They put up a huge high-tech mast on top of the hillside: *my* hillside. I love that hillside; it's my favourite place in the whole world. There's enough space to run and practise cartwheels or just sit and look at the view. I don't go near the edge. I'm not stupid. But you know what? After the mast was built, I kind of forgot it was there half the time.

The day of the official opening of the CyberSky headquarters, I was down in the town with Mum and my brother Joe and my best friend Imogen. Mum was holding a big sign on a wooden post. It said

DON'T RADIATE MY KIDS!

She and her friend Nicky are always protesting about something: rainforests, whales, banks. Nicky is one of the shoutiest people in Bluehaven. This time they were complaining about the phone mast being so close to the town (which it wasn't really) and they'd persuaded about twenty people to come along and protest too. Joe and I always find it SO embarrassing. 'Dad would never turn up to this,' Joe muttered.

Dad's in the army and he's abroad a lot. He says mobile phones and the masts are perfectly safe and that all this worry about radiation is a complete over-reaction from people who believe everything they read online. It's one of the few things he and Mum argue about when he's home. He thinks she gets all riled up about silly stuff. Sometimes I think Mum's right to get mad about things. I mean, if no one ever made a fuss, nothing would ever get changed, would it? I just wish she didn't have to drag us into it. I don't like being the centre of attention.

There were plenty of other people there too— people who thought that the new company would be good for the area and create lots of jobs—plus the Bluehaven mayor, Mr Foley, who was nearly bald but tried to pretend he wasn't by wearing a wig.

'We could sneak off and go buy ice cream,' Joe muttered. 'No one would notice.'

I was tempted. 'Have you got any money?'

He sighed. 'Spent it all on the new Batman figure.'

My brother is OBSESSED with superheroes. He makes his own films and collects comics and figurines. Sometimes he talks to them as if they're real people, when he thinks no one can hear him. Which is kind of sweet but also kind of *disturbing*.

Imogen was gazing up at the CyberSky building. She's taller than me and has long brown hair that she wears in a plait. 'It's almost like it can make itself invisible,' she said. 'You know? All those glass windows, like mirrors. They reflect the sky so that it almost looks like the building isn't really here.'

I looked up too. 'Er . . .' I said. It was a building; you couldn't get away from that. Tall and square, like it belonged in a city business area or something. But Imogen has this way of looking at things differently. She pulled out a sketchpad and a pen from her bag (she's never without THEM) and started drawing the building. I watched over her shoulder, marvelling. My buildings haven't progressed beyond the infant stage: two vertical walls, a triangular roof, a door and square windows, and a chimney on top. If I have time, I'll colour the roof in red. *That's* the extent of my artistic abilities. But Imogen is really amazing. Within seconds, she'd sketched and shaded in the building so that it looked like it was made of clouds and sky. Watching her draw, I understood what she meant about the building almost being invisible.

Joe nudged me. 'Look, someone's coming out.'

The front doors had opened, and a woman in a grey suit walked out into the sunshine. She was pale, with grey hair in a shiny bob and grey shoes. She looked like the sort of person who stayed out of the sun. Her name was Professor Macavity and she ran CyberSky. I knew that because her photo had been in the paper for months. Mr Foley stepped forward, mopping his shiny brow. His mayoral chain glinted. His wig blew up in the breeze and exposed a bit of bald patch.

'CyberSky out!' shouted the thin line of protestors. Nicky's voice was the loudest. 'Don't radiate our kids!' Mum went, 'Yeah!' and waved her placard aggressively. Joe and I tried to hide behind Imogen.

Mr Foley shook the professor's hand and nodded and smiled. The professor (nodding but not smiling) went to a microphone set up just in front of the doors. 'Good morning,' she said, and for a moment, my heart went THUD because she *sounded* grey too. I'm not kidding. Her voice was like a cold wind on a grey day. It made me SHIVER.

She said how pleased she was to be here (she didn't sound pleased) and how welcoming the residents of Bluehaven had been (which wasn't really true, especially not Nicky and my mum) and how CyberSky was at the forefront of technology development (which, according to Imogen's dad, who reviews gadgets for his job, *is* actually true). It was all very boring. But *then* she said something that made me **SQUEAK** with excitement . . .

'As a thank you, CyberSky will be delivering a free mobile phone to every resident over the age of ten in Bluehaven, along with six months' free calls and internet services.'

Imogen and Joe **SQUEAKED** a bit too, and Imogen even put her sketchbook away. 'A brand new phone! **EACH**!' My brother is just ten. He looked like he was about to explode with happiness.

Nicky shouted, 'We don't want your filthy phones!' but some of the protesters were looking a bit uncertain now. After all, a free phone is a free phone.

And then the mayor said something and someone cut a ribbon, and my mum put a supportive arm around Nicky and muttered

something about not giving up the fight, and we went home. And Imogen and Joe and I chatted ALL THE WAY about the brand new phones we were going to get.

IF ONLY I'D KNOWN THEN WHAT I KNOW NOW . . .

CHAPTER 2

The new CyberSky phones were **AWESOME**. They looked massively expensive, and weighed almost nothing. PLUS they had fingertip recognition software, so no one but you could get into the phone. When mine arrived, I spent ages looking through all the pre-loaded apps and playing the games. My favourite was one about a pack of lemmings who were going to end up jumping off a cliff if you didn't build walls and ditches to herd them into the safe zone. The only app I didn't get was called **QuizTime**. The questions were off-the-wall crazy. Like this one:

How can you throw a ball as hard as you can and have it come back to you, even if it doesn't bounce off anything? There is nothing attached to it, and no one else catches or throws it back to you.

Joe had to tell me the answer to that in the end, and it made me feel really stupid (and if you can't work it out either, you'll find the answer at the bottom of this page).[1]

Imogen totally aced QuizTime. I was surprised; she doesn't like tests at school, though she always does fine. But she got *really* into them, so much so that when she reached into her bag now, it'd be for the phone, not her sketchbook. 'Level seventeen!' she exclaimed a week later at school, her round face shining with delight.

'Seventeen? Really?' I'd given up at level five, preferring to save my pack of lemmings from a watery death. '**WOW!** How are you doing it?'

'I don't know. They're just my kind of questions, that's all. Like this one.' She held out the phone.

There are three boxes. One is labelled 'APPLES', another is labelled 'ORANGES'. The last one is labelled 'APPLES AND ORANGES'. You know that each box is labelled incorrectly. You can pick one piece of fruit from one box only to help you decide how to re-label the boxes.

1 Answer: throw the ball straight up in the air.

'What?' Even reading the question made my head hurt.

Imogen beamed. 'It's easy once you know the answer. You pick one fruit from the APPLES AND ORANGES box. If it's an apple, then you change the ORANGES box to APPLES AND ORANGES, and the APPLES box to ORANGES. See?'

'What?' I said again. 'How did you figure it out?'

'I don't know. I just see it in my mind, you know? Like I can see the boxes sitting in front of me, and I sort of imagine reaching out and taking something out of one of them . . . ' She yawned and rubbed her eyes. 'I stayed up a bit too late last night trying to figure it out. It was worth it to get to the next level though.'

'Wow.' I watched her tapping away at the screen for a moment more, trying to understand why anyone would want to stay up late answering quiz questions. Then, because I was feeling like a bit of a spare part, I said, 'Oh, I forgot to tell you. Mum says we can get Mexican on the way home from **XSCAPE** on my birthday.'

That made Imogen look up. 'Cool! I love burritos.' Then she went back to her phone.

I was a bit disappointed she didn't want to talk more about my birthday because I was REALLY excited. I was going to be twelve in another six weeks! And Mum had said I could bring Imogen along for my treat. It'd be me and her and Mum and Joe (I didn't really mind him tagging along because he was mostly OK when he wasn't talking to his superhero toys.)

XSCAPE is this *amazing* indoor ski slope near us. I'd never been skiing before, so I was really looking forward to it. Imogen and I had looked at the website and planned what to wear and how we'd deal with looking stupid when we fell over. We'd even practised our 'I totally MEANT to do that' faces.

'Hey!' I said to Imogen, pulling out my own CyberSky. 'I had another idea. We can use the camera on this to video each other coming down the slopes!'

'Mmm,' she said, not looking up.

I switched on the camera app and had a go at videoing the playground. You could zoom in really close and the quality was brilliant. I even caught a bit of Scarlett May, the Year Nine super-bully, doing her I-am-queen-of-the-school thing. Scarlett has dyed blonde hair and big blue eyes and looks like an angel. Never be fooled by appearances. Inside she's got the personality of an **ASIAN GIANT HORNET** and the venom to match.

Scarlett hangs around with Emma and Jasmine and the three of them are the people you would least like to meet in a dark alley. Or in a light alley. Or any alley anytime, come to that. Today, they were picking on a couple of Year Eight girls across the playground. I couldn't hear what they were saying, but by zooming in I could see one of the Year Eights turning away, looking miserable. I felt a bit sick and switched off the camera app. If only the teachers knew what Scarlett and her sidekicks were really like. But no one dared stand up to Scarlett.

I played the lemmings game for a bit but my legs were fidgety. I wished I had gym club every day instead of just twice a week. Imogen used to help me with my handstands at break when she wasn't drawing or doodling, but now she was always on QuizTime.

Over the next three weeks, the only time Imogen *didn't* have the phone in her hand was in lessons (and even then, I sometimes saw her sneak the phone under the table). She became completely obsessed with answering those weird questions! She looked a bit pale too and there were dark circles under her eyes.

I've got to be honest: as those three weeks passed, I started to feel a bit annoyed. It was as though I was invisible. 'Can't you put it down for a bit?' I said in the end.

'Hmm?' Imogen was staring at a quiz question and frowning. 'This has to be simpler than I think . . . '

'Imogen. Hello?' I waved a hand in front of her face.

'Don't do that, I'm concentrating,' she said. Her voice sounded flat.

I sighed. 'Look, we've been sitting here for twenty minutes and you've not spoken to me once.' (I tried not to sound whiny, I really did, but it might have been a little bit whiny. Tiny whiny.)

'Ah!' Imogen tapped something on her phone and the screen lit up with GLITTERING FIREWORKS. 'That's it! Of course! Why didn't I think of it before?' She put the phone into her pocket. 'What's the matter?'

'Talk to me,' I said. 'Are you going to come on that activity course in the summer holidays?

The one with the quad bikes and the tennis?'

'Oh, I don't know yet,' she replied. Her voice was all flat again, like she was completely uninterested. 'I haven't thought that far ahead.'

I didn't know what to say next. This NEVER used to be a problem for us! Imogen and I always talked loads and loads in the past, with no awkward silences or anything. But there was one now. 'Um . . . ' I said, trying to fill it. 'How's that painting you were doing? The one of the beach—have you finished it yet?'

'The painting?' She was staring out at the playground. 'Oh—no. No, I haven't finished it.'

Another dead end to our chat. I felt frustrated. Even though she was talking to me, it was like she wasn't properly here. 'Why do you like these quizzes so much?' I asked eventually.

She turned to me and smiled. 'They make me think. But differently from how I have to think at school. It's like my brain kind of *knows* what to do, to twist the problem, turn it inside out, so I can look at it from all angles.' Her smile grew wider. 'And each time I get the right answer, I feel really good. You know?'

'Er,' I said, but not because of what she'd said. Something inside me THUMPED uncomfortably, because the smile—the smile she was smiling now—wasn't quite right. How can I explain? It wasn't her usual smile. A smile's a smile, you'd say—but no. There are different kinds of smiles. And this one was kind of **WEIRD**.

But then she pulled out her phone again and the smile vanished, and she wasn't talking to me any more anyway. I wasn't sure whether to feel angry or relieved. So I settled on frustrated.

That afternoon we had a visit from Professor Macavity in Lower Assembly. Mrs Lester, the Head, looked so excited she was practically **LEVITATING**. Usually the most interesting person who came to talk to us was PC Sara Goodwill, who reminded us how to cross the road safely and not to vandalize public property.

'I want complete attention,' Mrs Lester told us, as we sat on the plastic chairs (you know, the ones that make your bottom sweat, especially on a hot day). 'Professor Macavity has very generously agreed to give up her valuable time to come and talk to us about the future of mobile phone technology, so I want everyone to be on their best behaviour.'

The professor stood at the front of the hall, her arms crossed, her expression blank. She was wearing the same grey suit she'd worn on the day of the CyberSky opening, or maybe she had loads of identical grey suits. She looked like an angular grey cloud. An ominous one. I gave a twitch of unease. She was **TRULY CREEPY**.

'Good afternoon,' she said, in that flat voice. Her gaze swept over the four hundred or so kids in the hall. 'As you already know, I am the Chief Executive Officer of CyberSky. I trust you have all received your new phones.'

There was a cheerful mumble from the audience. I glanced at Imogen, who was sitting next to me. For once, she didn't look as though her thoughts were somewhere else. Her eyes were fixed intently on the professor. Like, properly *fixed*. Like they were glued to the storm cloud. 'Hey.' I nudged her. '*Hey.*' She didn't even register me. I felt even more uneasy.

'Technology is the past, the present and the future,' Professor Macavity said. 'The human race has always looked to exploration and discovery . . . '

I lost interest after a few minutes. Her voice was so difficult to listen to! And it was as though she'd forgotten who her audience was. We were a bunch of schoolkids, not some group of business people in suits like hers. She used a lot of long words, and I'd swear some of them were made up. What's '*analogue*' when it's at home?

Imogen hung on her every word, her eyes big and round, not even a hint of a yawn. I was baffled. I sneaked glances around the room and was relieved to see that most others looked as bored as I felt. Scarlett and her two pets were sitting three rows ahead of me and were whispering together and giggling. I felt some sympathy. I'd have been whispering to Imogen if she'd let me!

There were several other kids staring at Professor Macavity like she was some kind of god. Malia Brunt, the other side of Imogen, had the same glazed look of concentration. I was surprised because Malia's a total bookworm and loves history. She told me once she wished she lived in Victorian times. So in a way, I was kind of surprised she even knew what a mobile phone was! I sighed. Why was everyone so interested in technology suddenly? Malia and Imogen were the last people I'd expect to care! I just wanted to get up and *do* something. All this sitting around made me jittery.

'And so,' the professor said, varying her tone

a little so that I was hopeful she was coming to the end of her talk, 'the kind of people we need to advance our technology are those with highly unusual brains. People who can see beyond what *is* and into what *could be*. Visionaries. Flexible brains with infinite potential.'

I screwed up my nose. Flexible brains? Sounded disgusting! All floppy and slippery and . . . EWWW.

'Some of you . . . ' The professor paused. Her grey eyes scanned the room. 'Some of you may have the kind of brain we need. The brain that can connect the dots and make leaps of imagination.' Her gaze stopped dead, and for one frightening moment, I thought she was looking straight at me. I couldn't breathe. Her eyes! Like *lasers* or something, boring right through you! Unless . . . no, it wasn't me she was looking at . . . it was *Imogen*.

Imogen, staring straight back with that weird smile on her face.

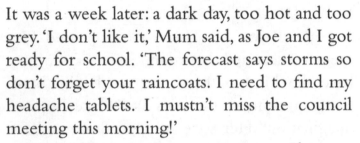

CHAPTER 3

It was a week later: a dark day, too hot and too grey. 'I don't like it,' Mum said, as Joe and I got ready for school. 'The forecast says storms so don't forget your raincoats. I need to find my headache tablets. I mustn't miss the council meeting this morning!'

Mum gets migraines sometimes. She says it's to do with atmosphere. Dad says it's because she gets tense about so many 'issues'. I don't know who's right but today even I felt like I had a headache. I didn't want to go to school. Not only did Imogen barely notice me any more, but she'd started to hang around with Malia Brunt. The two of them sat with their phones in their hands, staring blankly at the screens as their fingers tapped away at those stupid quizzes. It was **DEAD CREEPY,** and every time I tried to see her phone, Imogen lifted a shoulder and said in that monotone, 'Don't, Holly. I'm busy.' And so I sat next to her, because there wasn't anywhere else to go, gazing miserably at my feet and trying not to attract attention from Scarlett and her lot. Because if there's one thing that attracts bullies, it's the invisible word VICTIM hovering over your head. Along with LONELY and SAD.

Joe talked non-stop all the way to school. It was REALLY irritating, and it made my not-quite-headache start to turn into a Real One. He was chuntering on about ELECTRICAL STORMS and Frankenstein, and in the end I just snapped, 'What *are* you going on about?'

'It's the right kind of weather for it,' Joe said cheerfully.

'For *what*?'

'Animating a dead body! Like in the story. Doctor Frankenstein made a monster out of bits of people and then it was brought to life by lightning.'

'You're disgusting,' I told him. 'That's just vile.'

He shrugged. 'I didn't make it up, someone else did.'

'Well, *he's* vile then.'

'It was a girl, so there. Mary Shelley wrote *Frankenstein*.'

I stomped along. My brother was being all clever and know-it-all, though at least he was still talking to me. I wished I didn't have to go to school today. I wanted to go up to the hilltop and run really fast and do handstands and see how many cartwheels I could turn in a row. Someone at gym club could do five, and I was determined to beat her. But it was Thursday and I had a whole six and a half hours of school to get through. URGH!

Joe turned off at his school gates first, while I trudged on down the road, feeling kind of like a black cloud myself. When I got to my own school drive, the first person I saw was Imogen, talking to Malia. For once, they didn't have their phones in their hands, and they looked almost NORMAL. Well, when I say *normal*, I mean crazily happy. Practically squealing at each other and doing high-fives. Totally different from how they'd looked these past weeks.

'Hi,' I said, trying to catch Imogen's attention. 'What's going on?'

Imogen swung round and I was nearly knocked over by the enthusiasm of her smile.

It looked REAL, not the weird almost-smile she'd had. I felt my mouth curve up in response. 'Holly! I'm so glad you're here!'

My spirits lifted. 'Really?'

'I've got the most *amazing* thing to tell you!' She took my arm and I felt like crying with happiness. Though, I didn't, *obviously*, because that would be highly embarrassing. 'You know all those quizzes we've been doing, me and Malia?'

'Yes . . . ' My heart sank a little. That flipping QuizTime!

Imogen looked at Malia and the two of them shared manic smiles again. 'Well, our phones both went crazy last night at the same time— seven o'clock. The screens lit up with all these amazing patterns, flashing CONGRATULATIONS and YOU'VE WON! And then the phones rang!'

'Er . . . ' I said.

'It turns out it was all a giant competition!' said Malia. The last time I'd seen her this excited was when we'd visited a Roman villa. 'To find people with the right kind of brain! Exactly like the professor was saying the other day!'

I was baffled. 'What do you mean?'

Imogen turned to face me. 'CyberSky—they wanted to find twelve people with really imaginative brains, to test out their newest technology. So they put the quizzes on the new phones—and the people who get the furthest are invited to the **CyberSky HQ** next Saturday to try out this new top secret thing! And *both* of us have got in! Isn't that SO amazing?'

A chill swept through me. '*Next* Saturday? You mean in nine days' time?'

'Yes! I'm so excited!' She high-fived Malia again. 'It'll be like seeing into the future, all this new technology they're working on.'

'Yeah!' Malia nodded enthusiastically. 'And maybe we'll get stuff to bring home, like in a goody bag?'

'I want to know if they're going to put chips in people's heads,' said Imogen. 'Like in films. So you won't even need a phone in the future.'

'But Imogen,' I said, in a really small wobbly voice, 'next Saturday is my birthday. We're going to **XSCAPE**.'

She didn't hear me. 'Cos you know in films, the stuff they think up—well, in another ten or twenty years it turns out to be true. My dad was saying . . . '

'Imogen,' I said again, trying not to cry, 'next Saturday is my birthday. You can't go to CyberSky.'

That got her attention. She swung round. 'This is a once-in-a-lifetime opportunity, Holly. Of course I have to go. Your birthday happens every year.'

I was speechless. How could my best friend say something like that? We'd been planning this *for months!*

There was a simultaneous beeping, and both Imogen and Malia pulled out their phones. As they looked at the screens, their faces went completely blank, just as they did when they were playing QuizTime. It was seriously freaky.

Then, without another word, both of them just turned and walked away.

I found my voice. 'How *could* you?' I yelled. 'How could you let me down?'

But Imogen didn't look back. Her gaze was fixed on her phone as she and Malia walked side by side into school.

I watched them go, my eyes full of tears and my throat full of words I couldn't say.

CHAPTER 4

HOLLY'S SADNESS DROVE HER TO THE HILLSIDE AFTER SCHOOL.

BUT TODAY WAS NO ORDINARY DAY. AN IMPOSSIBLE BALL OF LIGHT WAS SKIMMING OVER THE WATER TOWARDS HER!

My hair stood on end; my fingers tingled. I stood **FROZEN** to the spot, wishing so hard that I'd done something different to keep my friend.

A strange **BUZZING** noise filled the air, like a swarm of bees. Then the light streaked over my head, crashing into the grey globe on top of the CyberSky mast, and **EXPLODING** into a brilliant shower of green sparks.

HOLLY BREATHED A SIGH OF RELIEF THAT THE LIGHTNING HAD MISSED HER—AND THEN AN ARC OF ELECTRICITY SHOT OUT FROM THE SIDE OF THE GLOBE STRAIGHT AT HER!

SCHWUMPZZ

HOLLY WAS UNCONSCIOUS BUT INSIDE HER BRAIN, CHANGES WERE TAKING PLACE . . .

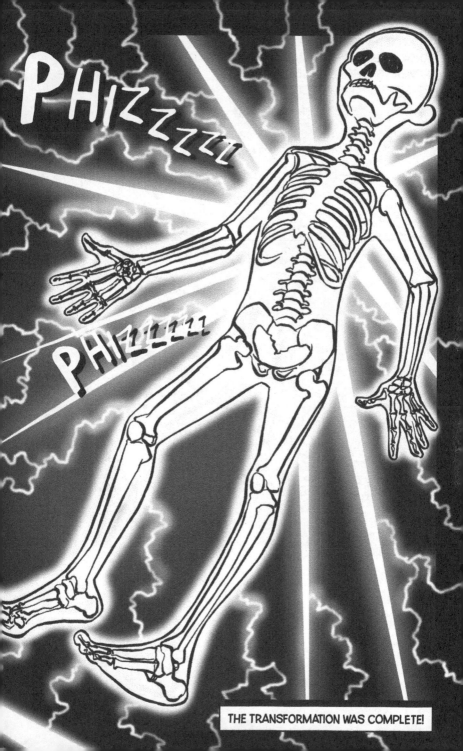

BUT FOR THE MOMENT, HOLLY KNEW NOTHING OF THE AMAZING POWERS SHE HAD BEEN GIVEN . . .

I don't know how long I lay on the grass unconscious. When I woke up I felt . . . odd. Different. A bit achy. And kind of PRICKLY all over.

Oh, and wet. It was raining.

It felt like a very long walk home. My chest hurt a bit, and I kept rubbing it. What had happened? Had I actually been hit by lightning? Was that what it was like? I mean, people *can* be hit by lightning, can't they, but—me? Holly Sparkes? In Bluehaven, England? SERIOUSLY?

Or had I imagined the whole thing? Lightning comes down from the sky in a jagged arrow, not whizzing sideways like a meteor, bouncing off phone masts and turning green. It can't have been lightning. Had I got so worked up about Imogen that I'd, I dunno, tripped and hit my head, and imagined a whole load of surreal stuff about balls of light and green sparks and . . . ?

The more I thought about it, the less real it seemed. By the time I got home, I felt completely exhausted and more than a bit shaky. What was I going to tell Mum? I had no idea what the time was; my watch had stopped.

She was looking out for me. When she opened the door, I wanted to run into her arms and sob everything out—but she made a clicking noise with her tongue and said, 'Thank goodness you're back! You're wet through, darling, you should get out of those clothes straight away. Go and get in the bath, all right? Goodness, I was worried about you.' Then she stepped forward, gave me a quick hug and a kiss on the cheek, and turned to go, saying, 'Nicky and I are planning a video protest about the effects of mobile phone masts near schools; the council thought it might be a good idea. We might ask you and Joe to do some acting! I'm in the kitchen if you need me!'

I watched her go, unable to speak; to say, 'I do need you, Mum! Please give me a proper hug and tell me that people are absolutely fine after they've been hit by **WEIRD GREEN LIGHTNING!**' But she was busy—and anyway that sounded insane! I just needed to pull myself together, that was all.

I peered into the living room. Joe was sitting on the floor, cutting out a large shape from a piece of cardboard. It looked a bit like a block of flats. Probably something for one of his homemade superhero films. He was busy too. Everyone was busy. I should just go and have a bath, like Mum suggested. So I left the room without saying anything.

I dragged myself up the stairs to my bedroom. The skies outside were so dark! I felt all heavy and **PRICKLY**, especially my fingers. I reached out for the light switch ...

I was *so tired*. I chucked my wet clothes into the basket by my door and put on my pyjamas. I didn't have the energy for a bath. Instead, I got into bed and pulled the duvet up to my neck. It felt *good* to be lying down, closing my eyes.

It might have been seconds or minutes later that I heard my brother's voice from the doorway. 'Holly, can you come and help me for a minute?'

'No,' I said. 'Go away.'

'Why are you in bed? Are you sick?'

'I'm just really tired, Joe.' I made my voice as **UNWELCOMING** as possible.

He stayed put. 'Oh, *please*. I'm filming a scene. I just need you to hold the camera while I do it.'

'Use the tripod,' I said unhelpfully.

'I can't get the right angle.'

Argh! 'Joe, I'm *really* tired.'

'It'll only take two minutes, honest.' His voice had gone all wheedling and nicey-nicey.

I gave a big sigh and threw back the duvet. 'Oh, all *right*.'

His room was draped in white bedsheets, and on a low table by the wall, he'd built a cardboard set. There were house fronts and a big domed building that looked a bit like a cathedral. I also spotted the tower block he'd been cutting out downstairs. In front of the cathedral, Batman and the Penguin were lying on their backs, gazing blankly up at the ceiling.

I smiled faintly. 'Batman and the Penguin having a showdown?'

'Yeah. It's the **BiG FiNALE.**' Joe got down on all fours and crawled under the table.

I picked up the video camera. 'Where do you want me to stand?'

'I need you to get quite low, so that you're looking up at them.' Joe pointed. 'If you kneel there, and tilt it upwards a bit? I tried it from there and it was good. That way they look bigger and more impressive.'

I knelt down and frowned at the camera screen. 'Like this?'

'Yep . . . ' Joe wriggled his arms up around the side of the table and grabbed the two figures. 'Right, are you ready?'

'Yeah, all right.'

It was possibly the shortest battle scene in superhero history. Batman and the Penguin headbutted each other a couple of times, and Joe made obligatory groaning and yelling noises, and then the Penguin fell off the table completely and Joe called, 'Cut!' and grumbled about banging his elbow.

'I'll have to do it again,' he said, crawling out. His dark-blond hair was all sticking up on one side.

I stopped the camera recording and sighed.

'That's the fourth time you've sighed,' Joe said, checking that the Penguin still had both his flippers. 'Can you not do it while you're recording? It messes with the sound quality.'

'Look,' I snapped, 'I'm doing you a favour. Don't tell me not to sigh. *I've had a bad day.*'

'Yeah?' He carefully moved the cardboard tower block a little to the right. 'Do you think this would be better over here? Or was it OK where it was?'

I sighed again. 'I don't care, Joe.'

'You ARE in a bad mood.' He put on a stupid baby voice. 'Aww, poor Holly. Did Imogen take all your toys at playgroup?'

I couldn't speak. Imogen and I had been best friends for ever, and although we didn't always agree on everything, there was never any question that we'd stop being best friends. But now I had a horrible, horrible feeling that it was over. What would I do without her? There was a **PRICKLY** feeling in my chest and

MY

FINGERS

BEGAN

TO

TINGLE ...

HOLLY FELT UTTERLY MISERABLE.

I might try something different this time . . .

I can't believe Imogen doesn't care about me any more.

THE PRICKLY FEELING GOT WORSE . . . UNTIL SUDDENLY . . .

CHAPTER 5

What in nightmare's name was this thing on my neck?! It was **BRIGHT RED** and looked like some kind of fern, or one of those weird fractal pictures that they call 'magic eye', the ones that have a hidden picture inside the patterns. I pulled my shirt open and saw that the pattern spread right over the front of my body. But it was brightest just in the middle of my chest. Right over my **HEART**.

I felt sick and dizzy. This wasn't like one of Mum's migraines. Was there something wrong with my heart? Were my blood vessels poisoned or something? *OMG . . . ! Was I going to die?!*

And THEN—you won't believe this—it went. The pattern just . . . disappeared. Like it was never there. No red spidery marks— nothing.

Gone.

I blinked, and rubbed my eyes. There was nothing to see except the usual colour of my skin.

I gazed into my own eyes and took a deep breath. *You have to tell someone*, I could hear a voice in my head saying. *Something really weird is happening. You need help.*

I should tell Mum. But she was in the middle of a meeting with Nicky. I cringed at the thought of going into the kitchen and telling them I thought I'd been struck by lightning. Nicky would immediately blame the mobile phone mast. She'd probably insist on me speaking to the papers about how I nearly died or something. I *could* wait until she'd gone before telling Mum. But what was there to tell? There was nothing to see any more! She'd think I was barking mad!

Maybe I WAS actually going mad. Maybe this was a sign. Holly Sparkes has finally lost it. She can no longer tell what's real and what's not. They'd put me in a hospital and run tests on me and give me drugs, wouldn't they? Isn't that what happens on TV?

Joe was still banging on my door, and I heard him shout, 'Hey! You bust my camera!'

Oh no! If Mum heard . . .

I pulled the chair away from my door and opened it so quickly he practically fell into my room, furious. '*You bust my camera!*' he said again, holding it up resentfully. 'And what's that *thing* on your neck?'

I lifted my chin. My skin was clear. 'What thing?'

He stared. 'But . . . there was this red rash. Like . . . I dunno . . . '

'And it's not my fault the camera bust,' I went on. I felt all trembly, and cross *because* I was trembly. 'It just went bang in my hand. I could have been *seriously hurt.*'

He looked suddenly guilty. 'Are you hurt?'

'No,' I had to admit. 'No, I'm OK.' *Except I'm really not.*

'It didn't even burn you?' Joe asked in concern.

I held out my hand to show him. 'No. No marks.'

He stared. 'It blew up in your hand and you haven't got a mark on you? *That's lucky.*'

'Sorry about your camera,' I said. 'Is it completely dead?'

He held it out. 'I can't even get the card out. It's fused to the inside.'

I took the camera. He was right; the plastic casing had popped open and inside there was a kind of mass of melted plastic. It smelled horrible too. 'That's just . . . weird. Sorry. Did you have loads of stuff on the card?'

'No, just the scene we did today. I'd wiped it yesterday, so at least I haven't lost other stuff.' He chewed his lip. 'Mum's going to kill me, isn't she? It cost loads.'

'Maybe—er, well, we could not tell her yet. Find a good moment.' It sounded like I was waiting for a lot of good moments to talk to Mum. But I felt bad for Joe. Then I had an idea. 'Maybe you could use your CyberSky instead? It's got a good video function.'

He brightened. 'Yeah. Yeah, I might try that. Good idea.' Then he glanced at me curiously. 'You OK? You look a bit . . . you know. Ill.'

PANIC gripped me. Was I really, properly ill then? All the craziness in my head—did that show on the outside too? 'I'm fine,' I said, too quickly.

He looked at me for a second, as though he didn't really believe me. Then he shrugged. 'All right then. See you.'

I shut the door after he'd left and sat on my

bed. My head felt like it was buzzing with a million bees.

The voice in my mind kept whispering the impossible: *It was you. You broke the camera. You zapped the light switch. It's all you . . .*

But it CAN'T be, I wanted to shout back. Things like that don't really happen! Even after lightning strikes! People don't suddenly become electrified!

I was so, so tired. All this arguing with myself was getting me nowhere. Maybe when I woke up tomorrow, everything would be back to normal.

Tomorrow would be better, right?

ACTUALLY, TOMORROW TURNED OUT TO BE EVEN WORSE.

CHAPTER 6

I NEVER MEANT TO BLOW UP THE CLASSROOM.

Imogen and I always sit on the same table in maths, but on Friday I just couldn't bear the idea of sitting next to her. I couldn't forgive her for pulling out of my birthday and not even being *sorry* about it. I mean, what kind of best friend *does* that? I thought, if I sat next to her, I might actually cry. So I said, trying to keep my voice down so Imogen wouldn't hear me, 'Miss Howlett? Please can I sit somewhere else today?'

Miss Howlett (who looks like an owl, with these huge round glasses) was kind of stressed because we were supposed to be doing a test. 'Holly, don't mess around. Just sit down.'

'But Miss Howlett,' I said, '*please*. Me and Imogen . . . um.' I looked pleadingly at her. (Imogen was sitting at our usual table and staring down at her hands. I just *knew* she was playing with her phone, and that made it even WORSE.)

'Had an argument, have you?' Miss Howlett didn't look impressed. 'You'll just have to bite the bullet, Holly. I can't move everyone around now, there's no time. Go and sit in your usual place, please.'

I turned to the table, and Lottie and Ellen smiled at me encouragingly. But Imogen didn't look up at all and I couldn't—I just *couldn't*—sit there. 'Miss Howlett . . . ' I said miserably, 'I don't feel very well.'

Miss Howlett tutted in an irritated way. 'Oh, for goodness' sake, Holly. All right, go and sit at my desk. That's the only spare place in the room. You can do your test there.'

I tried not to notice the other kids staring at me as I made my way to the front of the room. My face felt hot with embarrassment. But I knew I'd rather sit at Miss Howlett's desk than next to Imogen.

There wasn't much room on Miss Howlett's desk. To my right was a laptop, connected up to the smartboard, and there were two big piles of paper and books taking up a lot of the space, along with pens and pencils and a calculator with extra-large keys. I pushed some things aside to make a space for my test paper.

Miss Howlett went round all the tables, handing out the test. 'You'll have twenty minutes to do this,' she said. 'Just do your best. No questions and no talking once we start.' She plonked a sheet in front of me. 'Better take this away,' she said, noticing the calculator. 'Right. You can start now.'

I picked up a pencil. I tried to concentrate on the questions, I really did, but I felt so sad. I couldn't help glancing over at Imogen. Did she *mind* that I wasn't sitting next to her? Or didn't she care at all? I looked over again—and she was looking right back. But there was nothing in her eyes. They were blank. It was like looking at someone who'd never met me. I felt a terrible coldness in my heart. It was over, then. My friend was no longer my friend.

Tears stung my eyes. My throat filled, and my chest burned, and my fingers tingled ... wait ...

OH NO! IT WAS HAPPENING AGAIN!

CHAPTER 7

I tried to explain to Miss Howlett, I really did. But she wouldn't listen. 'It's a **MALFUNCTION**,' she said, busy with the register. 'Some electrical fault. Now get in line, Holly, and be quiet!'

I didn't know what to do. I knew—just KNEW—that I'd done it all. Electricity had come blasting out of my hands! But who would believe that? I wouldn't have believed it if I hadn't seen and felt it! So I got into line and stayed quiet.

We were sent home, of course. The emergency services came to put out the fires and the smoke, and they told Mrs Lester that the school wasn't safe. They thought maybe it was a wiring problem, so the whole lot would have to be checked. Mum gave me the third degree when I got home. I could almost see her composing a letter to the school about health and safety in her head. 'Things just started blowing up by themselves?' she repeated in disbelief. 'And you all got covered in *broken glass*? Are you all right? Were you checked out by the doctors? I should probably take you to A and E!'

I decided that there would **NEVER** be a good time to tell her about my lightning strike. 'I'm fine,' I said hastily, stopping her reaching for her car keys. 'Honestly.' Which was kind of weird in itself, wasn't it? How could I have been next to so many **EXPLOSIONS** and not got hurt?

Mum insisted on examining my face and hair for 'cuts or bits of glass you might have missed'. She was relieved when she didn't find any. 'You'll be in shock, though,' she said firmly. 'You should have a rest.'

I did sit down on the sofa for a bit because I did feel really tired. It was almost as though whenever I got involved with electricity and things went bang, it took some of my energy away. Mum made me a cup of tea with sugar which I didn't really want but I drank it anyway and felt better. By the time Joe got home from school, I was outside on our trampoline, practising a routine I'd learned at gym club.

News spreads fast in our town. 'You **TOTALLY** have to tell me what happened!' he demanded.

I did two somersaults before saying, 'I already told Mum. Go and ask her.'

I should have known this wouldn't put him off. Joe plonked his bag at the foot of the ladder and stared up at me eagerly. 'Was it your classroom?'

'Yes.' I concentrated and then went through the routine again, hoping he'd go away.

He didn't. 'What happened? Tell me everything! Dev said his brother said the ceiling fell down on everyone!'

I mis-timed my somersault and landed on my head. 'Ow. Of course the ceiling didn't fall down, that's stupid. Stuff exploded, that's all.'

'**Stuff EXPLODED**?' My brother opened his mouth to go on, and then shut it. He stared at me very hard. 'Did it MELT, by any chance?'

Caught off guard, I glanced guiltily at him.

His eyes widened. '**Holly, what did you do?**'

Panic rushed through me like a wave. 'Not so loud!'

'Right, I'm coming in.' He clambered up the ladder, pushed through the net and joined me on the trampoline, where he sat cross-legged and gave me another hard stare. 'Tell me everything.'

I hesitated. 'You won't believe me.'

'I believe all kinds of stuff. Try me.'

'It's crazy,' I said. 'It's impossible. It's not real.'

Joe raised his eyes to the sky. 'For goodness' sake, Holly! I *live* in the not real, remember? *Impossible is my middle name!*'

'No it isn't,' I snapped. 'It's Andrew.'

He gave me that patronizing look that grown-ups give kids when they think they haven't understood a joke. 'Come on. Tell me. I can take it. And I *saw* you, remember? I was *there* when you melted my video camera.'

I deflated like a balloon. 'I'm really sorry about that. It was a complete accident.'

'How did you do it?' He put on a sympathetic look.

I hesitated. But I *badly* needed to tell someone, and Mum was just too big a risk. Imogen didn't care, so Joe was my only option.

I sat down opposite him and gave a sigh. 'Look, you can't tell anyone, all right?'

'Cross my heart and hope to die,' he said cheerfully.

'Don't say that!' I exclaimed, appalled. 'Being around me is kind of dangerous right now.'

His eyes gleamed. 'Cool! Tell me everything.'

So I did. And it was a *big* relief to be able to share it. I explained about Imogen getting addicted to QuizTime, and how she'd become all distant and weird. And how she wasn't going to come on my birthday trip, and I'd been really upset and gone up to the hillside. And how this light had appeared in the sky and . . . well, you know all of this anyway.

I told him about the classroom too. By the time I'd finished, my brother's eyes were bigger than dinner plates. 'WOW,' he breathed. 'You are SO LUCKY.'

I gave a disbelieving snort. 'Lucky?! I nearly killed everyone!'

He shook his head. 'You don't understand. You've got SUPERPOWERS.'

I tried to laugh but it sounded really false. 'Superpowers! Me? You've been reading too many comics, Joe.'

'No, I haven't,' he retorted. 'But this is totally unfair! Why *you*? Why should *you* be struck by lightning and turn into ELECTRO when *I'm* the one who knows all about superheroes?! It's *wasted* on you!'

'You totally don't want this,' I told him, meaning it. 'It's dangerous. I'm dangerous. What if—what if I *kill* someone by mistake? With—you know—*my powers*?' It still sounded SO silly to my own ears! My *POWERS*?! WHAT?!!

'That's why you need a mentor,' he said. 'Someone to help you learn to control it.' His eyes gleamed. 'HEY—can I be your mentor? Oh *please*! Holly, please say I can!'

I stared at him. 'You are *kidding*, right?'

Now he looked hurt. 'I know EVERYTHING about superheroes, remember? You need someone to watch your back, someone to help you train. *Please* let me do it!'

I tried to deny it one last time. 'I am *not* a superhero! You're insane!'

'Oh, come *on*!' Joe lost his temper. 'You can blow stuff up and melt things! Of *course* you've got SUPERPOWERS! It's JUST like what happened to Electro: struck by lightning, a classic origins story—it's not even *original*.' Joe looked vaguely disappointed for a moment.

'I was struck by something bouncing off the phone mast,' I corrected him. 'Not ordinary lightning.'

'Well, *duh*. Ordinary lightning doesn't come swooping over the sea like a shooting star. Though maybe'—he suddenly sat up straighter—'maybe it's not the light itself but the thing it bounced off. Maybe the mast warped the light in some way. Whoa! Maybe the mast IS full of radiation, like Mum's always going on about! You've been radiated by magic lightning!'

If I could have rolled my eyes any more obviously, I would have. 'Like I said, too many comics,' I said pointedly.

'Truth is often stranger than fiction,' he said, giving me a proper conspiracy theory look.

'This is ridiculous.' I got up. 'You're talking like a **CRAZY PERSON**.'

'Yeah?' He got up too, challenging. 'And *you* just blew up your classroom without touching anything. So who's the crazy one?'

I opened my mouth to reply but couldn't think of a single thing to say, so I shut it again.

'Please let me help you,' Joe said again, sounding more sympathetic. 'Let's face it, you can't tell anyone else.'

I looked down at my hands. 'Maybe I should go to the doctor.'

'**NO!**' Joe suddenly shouted with a force that shocked me. 'Don't **EVER** go to the doctor! They'll cut your head open and *dissect your BRAIN!*'

'Um . . . OK,' I said, alarmed. 'Chill, Joe.'

'I think,' he went on, 'you're a human EMP.'

'A what? What's an EMP?'

'Electro–Magnetic Pulse. It's like your body generates a huge amount of electricity and blasts everything around it. It's a real thing. The military uses EMPs as weapons.'

I didn't like the idea of being a weapon. 'I don't want it, Joe.' Suddenly I felt really upset. My lower lip wobbled, which was kind of embarrassing. 'I'm nearly twelve, not twenty-two. I'm not grown up enough to deal with this kind of thing. I just want to go back to being normal.'

'Hey.' My brother's voice was unexpectedly kind. 'It'll be OK. But you can't go back. You can't switch it off. It's a gift that comes with responsibility.'

My eyes filled with tears. 'I don't want responsibility.'

He leaned towards me. 'Holly, let me help you. I'm the only person who can.'

He was right. He *was* the only person. And considering that my only option was my ten-year-old brother, I think that says a lot about my life at that moment.

'All right,' I said, giving in at last. 'But I'm totally going to regret this.'

CHAPTER 8

In superhero films, they often condense the bit where the hero learns how to use his powers into some kind of montage. You know, you see bits of training where initially they're rubbish and then they get good, kind of quickly, usually with a catchy pop song. This is a book, so I can't do the pop song bit. But maybe you could listen to one while you read the next bit, and then you'll get the right kind of effect.

I began training the very next day: Saturday. Joe selected my bedside lamp and put it in the middle of the floor. 'Right,' he said. 'See if you can switch it on using your powers.'

I felt daft. 'I don't know how.'

'Concentrate,' he told me. 'It's probably to do with mental focus. **FEEL THE POWER.** Summon the electricity.'

I stretched out my hand towards the lamp,

staring at it. I tried talking to it in my mind. Switch on! Switch on!—but nothing happened. 'I can't feel anything,' I told Joe. 'Except embarrassed. This is silly.'

'You have to stop thinking like that,' he said sternly, 'or we'll never get anywhere. Do you WANT to keep losing control and blowing up your classroom? Cos it'll get you expelled.'

'Oh, all right,' I said. 'I *am* trying.'

Joe hesitated. 'You said that in the classroom, you were feeling sad about Imogen. Maybe that's the trigger. You need to feel really sad. Focus on the moment when Imogen told you she wouldn't come to your birthday.'

So I did. I thought about everything that had led up to it: Imogen's obsession with QuizTime, feeling like I was invisible, then the moment outside the school when she'd told me about the visit to CyberSky, and how—just for a second—I'd thought she remembered I was her best friend again . . . and then she threw it all in my face . . .

MISERY SWEPT THROUGH ME. PINS AND NEEDLES BEGAN TO PRICKLE MY FINGERS . . .

GRADUALLY, HOLLY LEARNED HOW TO BRING HE
POWERS UNDER CONTROL . . . AND DISCOVERED
THAT THEY COULD BE KIND OF FUN!
ZZZP!
Yay! I turned it on without blowing it up!
WHIRRRRR

THEY WENT BACK TO THE PLACE IT ALL BEGAN
I still don't understand what happened that day.
It was a million-to-one chance.
I just remember
hat weird light . . .
I think it was ball lightning. It's really rare.
You're so lucky!

School was closed on Monday while the electricity people checked all the wiring, so I had an extra day to practise (as long as I didn't do it while Mum was around) before I had to go back on Tuesday. I felt a bit better about my powers, although I was still nervous about LOSING CONTROL. At least I wasn't blowing so much stuff up by accident now. Joe kept reminding me that all I needed to do was to concentrate and breathe. 'You can switch your powers on and off whenever you like if you just FOCUS.'

The trouble was, the first person I saw at the school gates was Imogen—and straight away, I felt really sad. Her gaze passed over me as though I wasn't even there. Malia was standing with her. I blinked very hard to hold back tears. I kept breathing though. I didn't want my fingers to start tingling again! I walked quickly into school, trying not to look at her.

I sat with another group of friends at lunch break, but it wasn't the same. I missed her so much.

Mum was sympathetic but no help. 'Give her time,' she advised. 'You two have been friends for years. I'm sure it'll sort itself out.'

I wasn't sure at all. And I wanted SO BADLY to share my incredible secret powers with my old friend. I could switch on the TV from the other side of the room—without the remote! I could change station on a radio just by pointing my fingers at it! (All right, so that last one I'd only managed once, and the other two times had been sort-of disastrous . . .) But every time I saw Imogen, I knew I was in danger of losing control. Once or twice my fingers tingled so hard I had to excuse myself from the classroom and go and hide in the toilets until I'd calmed down again. It was exhausting and it made me cross and fed up.

By Thursday I was really grumpy from trying to keep everything in all the time. And so, in the playground at lunchtime,

I DID SOMETHING MONUMENTALLY STUPID.

CHAPTER 9

Everyone dreams of taking down the school bullies, right? So maybe it wasn't SO bad, what I did? Just bear that in mind before you read on ...

Remember Scarlett and her beautiful advert-perfect hair and her two BFFs? On Thursday, the three of them were in the corner of the playground, whispering and tapping at their phones. I didn't take much notice of them because I was too busy trying very hard not to glance across at Imogen and Malia, who were leaning against a wall not far from me, eyes fixed (as ever) on their phones.

I was sitting on a bench with Lottie and Ellen, who were discussing a TV show they'd watched the night before. (I hadn't seen it, so I couldn't really join in properly, but at least they included me.) Then Lottie nudged me. 'What?' I asked.

'Look.' She nodded in the direction of Imogen and Malia.

James Costello was walking towards them, clenching his fists and doing that kind of breathing when you're psyching yourself up. Lottie, Ellen and I watched, puzzled. James is the shortest boy in Year Seven. He's very sweet and quite shy and I didn't think I'd ever seen him start a conversation with *anyone* before, so I was GOBSMACKED when he said, out of the blue, 'Hi Malia.' Just like that. Like it was perfectly normal!

Malia didn't look up at first, so he said it again. Then she dragged her gaze away from her phone and frowned at him. She's quite a bit taller than James, so she was looking down. 'Yes?' she said. 'What is it?'

And then, out of the corner of my eye, I saw Scarlett, Emma and Jasmine detach themselves from the corner and approach slowly. Scarlett held up her CyberSky in front of her. What was she . . . oh no . . . was she *filming* James?

James hadn't noticed. Instead, he coughed and said to Malia, 'So . . . is tomorrow OK then?'

'Huh?' Malia's voice was flat. 'Tomorrow OK for what?'

'I was thinking of the cinema,' he said, his face

slowly turning bright red. 'Or maybe bowling. You can choose.'

I felt horribly sick, like something was crawling up from my stomach into my chest.

'Oh my God,' whispered Lottie. 'What does he think he's *doing*?'

Ellen put her hand over her eyes. 'I can't watch.' Then she peeped between her fingers.

Malia wrinkled her nose, baffled. 'What are you talking about?' Imogen, standing next to her, was still tapping at her phone. The old Imogen would never have ignored this!

Scarlett was closer now, only a couple of metres away, phone still held up steadily in front of her. Emma stifled a giggle. I wanted to shout to James, to warn him, but my breath stuck in my throat. I didn't want to get involved . . .

James shifted uncomfortably. '*You* know,' he said. 'Don't mess about.'

'No,' said Malia. 'I *don't* know.'

'You said you'd go out with me,' James said, but he was sounding less and less confident.

Malia's eyes opened wide and the detached look disappeared from her face, as though wiped off with a sponge. 'I said what?'

Ellen made a whimpering noise of

embarrassment. Lottie elbowed her in the ribs.

'D-didn't you?' James dug in his pocket and produced a crumpled piece of paper. His face was reddening. 'I got a note . . . I thought it was from you.'

Malia took it from him. 'That's not even my handwriting.' She stared at him, her mouth open. 'You fancy me? I mean, er, that's very nice of you and everything, but . . . well. I don't want to go out with you.' Then she added, 'Sorry.'

James's shoulders slumped. I didn't fancy him either but at that moment I just wanted to give him a hug. 'I am such an **IDIOT**,' he muttered. Then he sort of shrugged, as though he was trying to pretend he didn't really care, and rubbed a hand through his hair.

I knew what was going to happen just before it actually did. James turned away from Malia— and saw Scarlett, her phone held up just a metre or so from his head. He jerked backwards, **HORROR** spreading across his face. 'What are you *doing*? *Are you filming me?*'

Scarlett's mouth split into a wide smile. She tapped the screen of her own phone and said delightedly, 'Nice one, James. That's going straight onto YouTube.'

James and I both realized at the same moment what had happened. 'You wrote that note,' James said, his voice shaking with humiliation. 'You set me up!' Next to me, Lottie and Ellen gasped.

'Yep.' Scarlett tapped away and said. 'All uploaded! You're going **VIRAL**, thanks to CyberSky.' Then she burst out laughing, and so did Emma and Jasmine.

James looked like he was about to be run over by a tank and couldn't save himself. His face crumpled. I felt awful for him. It was one thing to be humiliated in the playground like that but quite another to have it shared with the world. And I just knew that by the end of the day, pretty much *everyone* in the school would have seen that video—and they'd be sharing it with *their* friends from outside school, and before you knew it . . .

Poor James.

I looked at Malia again. Wasn't she going to say anything? But Malia had turned away from James and the others and was staring at her phone again, though her face was definitely pinker than it had been. I couldn't blame her. Who would risk standing up to Scarlett?

How *dare* she? How *could* she humiliate people like that—for *fun*?!

MY FINGERS BEGAN TO TINGLE...

And then, without even planning it, I got to my feet.

CHAPTER 10

'I can't believe you did something so **STUPID!**' Joe exclaimed. 'Are you **COMPLETELY INSANE**? Do you want to have your head cut open and your **BRAIN DISSECTED**?'

'Oh, don't go over the top,' I snapped. 'I thought you'd be impressed! I used my powers for good! And it worked brilliantly! Scarlett was totally freaked out!'

'Holly,' said my brother, in an annoyed tone, 'when I said use your powers for good, I didn't mean give everyone in the school a demonstration!'

I said a rude word to him.

'Look,' he added, 'I think Scarlett got exactly what she deserved. And if you'd done it somewhere else, without a hundred witnesses, I'd have said well done. But you can't do stuff like that in public! Not without a disguise.'

I threw up my hands. 'I am **NOT** wearing tights and a cape!' To be honest, I already regretted the whole thing. Mrs Lester hauled me into her office along with Scarlett and demanded to know what had happened. Scarlett, a blubbering wreck, went on and on about the sparks she'd seen coming from my hands 'that, like, shot out and tried to **KILL ME**!'

I wanted to say she was an idiot and that I hadn't been trying to kill her at all, but I bit down hard on my tongue. My best defence was to look completely innocent.

Luckily, Mrs Lester didn't believe a word of it—which was predictable, since who would? I mean, who *actually* has real superpowers? 'Calm down, Scarlett,' she said in an exasperated voice (more than once). 'Holly, can you tell me what happened?'

I shrugged. 'I don't know, Mrs Lester. I was saying to Scarlett that she shouldn't have been horrible to James, and then her phone just sort of went **BANG**. Maybe it had a fault or something.'

'What did she do to James?' Mrs Lester's brow crinkled.

I was a bit hesitant about telling her, since Scarlett was sitting there giving me the evils and after all, I still had to face her in the playground tomorrow. And I didn't want to embarrass James and Malia—but on the other hand, Scarlett got away with way too much, didn't she? And I felt kind of powerful after what I'd managed to do to her phone. So I risked it. 'Scarlett wrote a note to James,' I said, 'pretending to be Malia and saying she'd go out with him. So James went to talk to her in the playground and she didn't know anything about it. And Scarlett filmed it and put it on the internet.'

Mrs Lester looked furious. 'Scarlett May, you deliberately filmed another student without their approval and put it online?'

Scarlett glared at me even more. 'Mrs Lester, Holly broke my phone! Isn't that what we should be talking about?'

'That's enough of that,' said Mrs Lester crisply. 'Holly, you can go to registration. Scarlett, you stay right here. I'll be making a call to your parents.'

I felt kind of proud of myself as I left Mrs Lester's office. Scarlett bullied so many people, it was nice to see her told off. But as I walked back to my classroom, anyone who saw me did a kind of double take. Then they turned to their friends and whispered excitedly. Three or four of them gave me broad smiles and thumbs-up signs as I passed.

By the time I reached my class, I felt really uncomfortable. I didn't like being the centre of attention. How many people had seen what actually happened? Surely only Scarlett and her two friends had been close enough to see the electricity jump from my hands to her phone. If others had seen, they wouldn't be smiling at me; they'd be freaked out, right? So they must just be pleased that I'd taken down the school bully. Which was nice, and I felt kind of proud about it, but at the same time I wished they weren't all looking at me.

So when my own brother had a go at me about it, I got cross. Because I knew he was right. 'OK, OK!' I said in exasperation. 'I get the point! I won't do it again.'

Having powers and not being able to show people was going to be **REALLY HARD**. I wished SO MUCH that Imogen and I were still friends!

'We need to find you a mission,' Joe said, shaking his head. 'A way of channelling your powers into making the world a better place.'

'I'm *ELEVEN*,' I reminded him.

'It doesn't matter. We just need to keep our eyes open for the right thing.'

I rolled my eyes.

But he was right.

AND MY MISSION WAS COMING CLOSER AND CLOSER, IF ONLY I'D KNOWN IT.

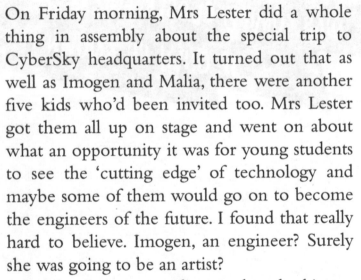

CHAPTER 11

On Friday morning, Mrs Lester did a whole thing in assembly about the special trip to CyberSky headquarters. It turned out that as well as Imogen and Malia, there were another five kids who'd been invited too. Mrs Lester got them all up on stage and went on about what an opportunity it was for young students to see the 'cutting edge' of technology and maybe some of them would go on to become the engineers of the future. I found that really hard to believe. Imogen, an engineer? Surely she was going to be an artist?

But Imogen was standing up there looking— well—*detached*, uninterested, as though her mind was somewhere else. Malia looked like that too. And as I gazed along the line of seven kids, I realized they *all* looked like that. A **CHILL** swept over me. What was going on? I remembered

Professor Macavity telling us *all* how important it was to have the right kind of brain to advance technology, and I shivered. Everyone up there . . . had something happened to their brains? Had something happened to Imogen's brain? Was *that* why she didn't want to be my friend any more?

I shook my head in disbelief. I'd been spending too much time with my comic-obsessed brother. These things didn't happen in real life. This was Bluehaven, for goodness' sake! The quietest, most boring town in the country!

Having powers had obviously given me an over-active imagination. Imogen just didn't like me any more. I didn't know why, but maybe I should try to get over it. Lottie and Ellen were nice. Maybe I should just be content to hang around with them.

The Saturday of my birthday was a good day. Mum drove me and Joe to XScape and it was **BRILLIANT**. I tried *very hard* not to miss Imogen, and some of the time I even convinced myself. Skiing was totally awesome and I instantly decided it was my favourite sport *ever*. 'Can we go skiing for *real* next year?' I begged Mum. 'Oh please, please, please?'

She gave me a half-smile. 'We'll see. It's very expensive. And such a dangerous sport too. I'm not sure I want my family racing down ice slopes at sixty miles an hour.'

'Dad's done skiing, hasn't he?' I said. 'In the army. I'm sure he did once.'

'Sand skiing maybe,' said Joe, slithering down the slope and falling with an undignified thump at our feet. 'He's always complaining about how hot it is.'

'Whatever. One day, we HAVE to go skiing for real. I'm going round again,' I announced, trying to get my feet to go in the same direction whilst the skis clacked together.

By the time we got to the Mexican restaurant, I was STARVING. And it had been a good day. Even though there was an emptiness in my heart where Imogen should have been. *I have other friends,* I told myself sternly. *I'm not going to mope around after someone who doesn't care about me any more.*

I *almost* convinced myself. But when we got home and heard the news, I knew I hadn't removed her from my heart at all.

CHAPTER 12

IMOGEN HADN'T COME HOME. She'd been at the ⊛CyberSky HQ and she hadn't been seen since. Everyone else had got home—but not her.

'But it's nine o'clock,' I said. 'Where could she be?'

Mum put the phone back in its holder. 'Her mum said that when she went to pick up Imogen from the CyberSky building, they said that Imogen had already left. Apparently she told them she'd walk home. But she never got there.'

I didn't know what to say. It was so impossible. No one ever went missing in Bluehaven. And Imogen—well, she was probably one of the most sensible people I knew! Where on earth had she gone? 'It must be a misunderstanding,' I said at last. 'She must have gone home with someone else.'

'That's why they rang here,' Mum said. 'To

see if she'd come to visit you.'

I looked around our hallway, even though I knew it was stupid. Imogen wasn't exactly going to be hiding under the stairs, was she?! 'Have they tried Malia Brunt?' I asked, even though saying it gave me a small pain inside. 'They're—friends.'

Mum shook her head. 'She's not there. None of the other kids who went to CyberSky have seen her since. They all left the building a bit earlier than expected at 4 p.m., even Imogen. But she hasn't rung anyone. No texts. Her mum's going mad. They've called the police.'

I felt very cold and very sick. The police? So . . . something must have happened to her. Something . . . something **BAD**.

'You'd better go to bed,' Mum said, seeing my expression. 'There's nothing we can do tonight. The police will find her, I'm sure.'

Go to bed? I knew Mum was right, but . . . how could I go to sleep when my best friend was missing? Suddenly, the great day I'd had came crashing down. And it was my birthday too.

I got to my room before I started to cry.

It was a very long night and I didn't sleep much. Joe came in at one point and sat on my bed and we chatted. Mum tried to tell us off but didn't have the heart. She made us hot chocolate instead. When I next woke up, Joe was curled up on the end of my bed snoring. I was glad to have the company.

I couldn't eat any breakfast. After I pestered her, Mum rang Imogen's house. 'Still no news,' she told me when she'd rung off. 'But her dad said the police are coming over here to ask you a few questions.'

'I don't know where she is!' I said, alarmed. Did they think *I'd* kidnapped her?

Mum smiled, though she looked kind of pale. 'They know you were friends, that's all. They'll probably want to know her favourite places, or any other friends she had, that kind of thing. Anything that might help them find her.'

I nodded, though I felt miserable as anything. 'We *were* friends. We're not now.'

Mum gave my shoulder a reassuring squeeze. 'Just tell them what you can.'

The inspector's name was Claire. 'Hello, Holly,' she said. 'I understand you and Imogen are best friends.'

'Not any more,' I said, trying not to sound pathetic. 'Not for a while.'

'Is she friends with someone else?' asked Claire.

'Malia,' I said. 'Well, sort of. They both love that QuizTime app.'

Claire nodded and grinned. 'I'm afraid I gave up at about question two. I don't think the right way. Your friend must be pretty smart.'

'Yeah, she is,' I said with a momentary flash of pride. 'She's *really* clever. She does these amazing drawings too—or at least, she used to. She's always on her phone now . . . '

'Her mother said the same thing,' said the inspector. 'She said Imogen was very excited about going to CyberSky.'

'Yes, she was.' That was the last time she gave me a real, genuine smile, I thought sadly. When she told me about the visit. 'She was really looking forward to it.'

Mum leaned over and squeezed my hand. 'Imogen should have been coming to Holly's birthday trip yesterday,' she told Claire, 'but when she won the competition, she pulled out.'

'Oh, that's a shame,' said Claire. 'I expect you were upset about that, weren't you?'

I nodded. 'Yeah. I mean, it was like she didn't care about me any more. I kept trying to talk to her, but she acted like I was **INVISIBLE** or something. All she cared about was her stupid phone. And her smile was all wrong.' I stopped, realizing that sounded *totally* weird.

Claire gave me a long look, and my stomach flipped with butterflies. But then she sighed in a sympathetic way, and asked me some more questions about Imogen's favourite places to visit, anything she'd said recently that had sounded unusual, or anyone she'd had an argument with. I hesitated but decided not to mention the thing with Scarlett, Malia and James at school. It wasn't anything to do with Imogen, and it might lead to awkward questions about what happened between me and Scarlett.

Eventually, Claire nodded and stood up. 'Thanks, Holly. I think that's all for now. Will you call me if you think of anything else that might be useful or if you hear from Imogen?'

'Are you out looking for her?' asked Mum in a quiet voice. I glanced at her. She was holding one hand to the side of her face, like she did when she got a headache.

Claire nodded. 'Yes. Everywhere she could possibly be. Don't worry. We'll find her, I'm sure.'

CHAPTER 13

Professor Macavity was on the local lunchtime news. She looked as grey and severe as ever. 'Imogen Clump was a very promising student,' she said to the camera. 'And here at CyberSky, we will do everything we can to aid the search for her.'

Joe scowled at the screen. 'They should be tracking her phone, that's what they should be doing. It's obvious.' He and I were sitting on the sofa together, eating crisps. Mum's headache had got worse and she'd taken a tablet and gone to lie down, hoping it would pass quickly.

'How do you track a phone?' I asked.

'Through a computer. The secret service can track any phone, anywhere, even if it's not switched on.'

'Really? In real life?'

He threw a crisp at me. 'Not everything you

read in comics is made up. Yeah, in *real life*.'
He said nothing for a moment, and then his
eyes narrowed. 'I wonder if . . . you could track
her phone yourself.'

'Me?' I stared at him. 'You just said you need
a computer.'

'Yes, but it's just sending information using
electricity, isn't it?'

I pulled a face. 'Sounds a bit advanced for
me. I mean, I've only just got the hang of not
blowing things up.'

'But your phone has made connections with
Imogen's before . . . ' said Joe as if thinking
out loud. 'I mean, you've texted each other
and stuff.'

'Yes, back when we first got them.'

'And maybe if you kept the idea of her phone
in your head while you fired electricity at your
own . . . I dunno. But it'd be worth a try, don't
you think?'

I fetched my phone from the kitchen and
held it in my hand. 'It'll be your fault if I blow
it up,' I told my brother.

He moved from the sofa to the other side
of the room. 'You just have to **FOCUS**, that's all.'

'Yeah? Why are you all the way over

there then?'

He shrugged and grinned. 'Safety first.'

I took a breath. 'I don't see how this is going to work. But I guess anything's worth a try.' Then I concentrated hard, and felt the TINGLING begin in my fingers . . .

HOLLY NEEDED FULL CONTROL OVER HER POWERS IF THIS WAS GOING TO WORK

BANG!

Focus . . . Control . . .

'*Oh pants!*' I stared at the broken phone on the floor.

'Shame,' said Joe, coming over. 'Another thing to add to the recycling pile.'

I sighed and bent to pick up the pieces. The back had come away completely, along with a couple of other plastic discs, revealing the battery and the SIM card, a tiny electronic circuit board, and something **WET** and **STRINGY**. 'Ew, what's this?'

Joe frowned. 'You melted it.'

'It's not plastic. It's . . . I dunno *what* it is.' I poked at the whitish stuff, and then nearly jumped out of my skin. 'It **MOVED**! Did you see that? That's just—URGH!'

'Let me see.' Joe knelt down next to it.

Trailing out of the phone was this—well, I don't know *what* exactly. It looked like a pile of **weird white worms**. It was very thin and kind of rubbery, and almost see-through. And it was *definitely* **TWITCHING**.

I took a step back, feeling sick. 'That is *disgusting*.' And then, something went 'PING' in my mind and I gasped. 'There was something like this in Scarlett's phone too! I saw it!' My mind flashed back to the day in the playground when I zapped the CyberSky. In my memory, I saw Scarlett dropping it, like she'd been stung, and the back snapping off—and this white stringy stuff . . . 'What *is* it?'

'Organic,' said Joe with authority. 'Something living. Wired into the phone.'

'That's just **WRONG**.'

'No,' he said, poking the quivering worms with enthusiasm. 'It's totally awesome. Technology with living matter. It's straight out of *Doctor Who*.'

'What's it doing there?' I asked, still staying well out of the way.

'I don't know. But it's wired into the phone, see?' He pulled at it, showing me that one end was firmly fixed to the circuit board.

'Don't touch it!' I said, trying not to gag.

'It's not poisonous.' He grinned with delight. 'It's *cool*. For all we know, this is the **future of technology**.'

'White worms? Yuck.'

'You said it was inside Scarlett's too. So it's likely this stuff is in every CyberSky phone.' He pulled at it, stretching it out to its fullest length, which was about thirty centimetres. The end attached to the circuit board came away with a snapping noise. The worms shuddered and then went completely limp.

'That is the **FREAKIEST THiNG** I have *ever* seen,' I said.

'It's only alive when it's attached to the phone,' mused Joe. 'Maybe the technology keeps it alive?'

I had an idea. 'Go get yours.'

'No fear,' he said with a snort. 'I'm not letting you bust mine as well.'

'But you don't want to use it if it's got this stuff inside it,' I pointed out. 'It could be doing anything: *sucking your brain out* or something!'

My brother was impressed. 'Now you're thinking like me!'

There was a noise from upstairs, and Joe hastily gathered up the pieces of the broken phone, including the wiggly worms, and jammed them into his pocket.

Mum staggered down the stairs. Her hair was a mess, and she had one eye screwed up against the light. 'Hey,' she said in a strained voice. 'Sorry, kids. This is getting worse, so I'm going to have to stay in bed the rest of the afternoon. You two can look after yourselves, can't you? Have you had lunch?'

'Crisps,' I said, guiltily.

'Eat something proper,' said Mum, trying to frown. 'Make a sandwich, or cook up a tin. There's some spaghetti if you want it.' She winced, turned and went back up the stairs,

Joe pulled out the white stringy worms from

his pocket. 'Spaghetti for lunch?' he said with a grin.

'*EWWW*,' I said in reply.

We made cheese and Marmite sandwiches instead. 'What are we going to do?' he asked.

'I can't stay in,' I said. 'I'll go mad. I know Mum told us not to go out, but . . . surely it's safe?'

Joe nodded. 'There'll be police everywhere. It's not as though we'd be kidnapped in broad daylight in front of them.'

I sat down with a thump. 'Do you think Imogen has been kidnapped?' My voice sounded small and a bit wobbly.

He pulled a face. 'What else could have happened?'

'I don't know. Maybe she's had an accident . . . ' My words trailed away. Suddenly, I'd lost my appetite completely. Was Imogen lying in a field somewhere, hurt and alone? The thought made me want to cry. 'We have to go out and look for her,' I said.

'Where?'

'I don't know. Anywhere. Everywhere.'

He looked at me for a moment and then nodded. 'All right. Maybe we can use your powers in some way too.'

'I'll write Mum a note,' I said, reaching for pen and paper.

'Eat first,' Joe told me sternly.

'I'm not hungry.'

'I'm your mentor and I say you have to eat,' he said. 'How are you going to fight crime on an empty stomach?'

It was so silly it made me laugh. 'You're an idiot,' I said fondly.

'Hey, I'm serious! You have to keep your strength up. It's important.'

I bit into the sandwich, still amused. My mentor? Joe sounded more like my mum!

CHAPTER 14

I was relieved to be out in the fresh air. The breeze was cool but not chilly, and the gulls squawked and fought each other in the sky. Out in the bay, the sea was choppy, with little white foamy caps to the waves. Joe and I walked in silence down the hill, both of us deliberately not glancing down the side road where Imogen lived. I felt really bad for her parents; they must be so worried.

My brain was racing with thoughts. Could Imogen have run away? But why? Had something happened at ⦿**CyberSky**? It was really weird that she'd disappeared just after that visit. She'd been looking forward to it so much. You'd have thought she'd race home to tell her parents all about it. Why had the visit finished early? Should we go and ask Malia? But the police had already spoken to her . . .

If Imogen had had an accident, she'd be somewhere near the main road. It wasn't that far a walk from her house to CyberSky—only about a mile. It was the only real practical thing we could do, so Joe and I walked the route down into town, keeping an eye out for anything unusual.

Then Joe **GROANED**. Coming up the hill towards us was Mum's friend Nicky. 'Holly and Joe!' she said in surprise, her wavy blonde hair falling across her face in the wind. 'Is your mum with you?'

'Er, no,' I said. 'She's got a migraine.'

Nicky's face fell. 'Oh no, the poor thing. I was on my way to see her. Thought we could set up an online action group to help coordinate looking for Imogen Clump.' She made a sympathetic noise. 'I guess that's what you two are doing, is it? Looking for her?'

'Yeah,' I said.

'You shouldn't really be out on your own, though,' Nicky said with a frown. 'I mean, if there are bad people about, it could be dangerous for you to wander around.' She glanced at her watch. 'I'll come with you.'

I shot a glance of **HORROR** at my brother. Nicky

was nice, but I didn't want to spend the afternoon with her! I still hadn't forgotten the time she'd told me the graphic details of whale hunting. I'd had nightmares for weeks. Even Mum had got cross with her about that. And I'd never be able to use my powers if she was tagging along.

Joe looked equally horrified. 'Er,' he said, and I could practically see his brain whirring. *Come on*, I thought. *You're better at thinking up stuff than I am!* 'That's really kind of you, but we're just going to stick to the main road. We figured it'd be safe. Actually, it's good we bumped into you. We've just come past the war memorial on Coronation Road, and someone should really check it out.'

'The war memorial?' asked Nicky, frowning. 'Why?'

Joe shrugged. 'There are a couple of kids with spray paint hanging around. I don't know if they're planning to use it, but . . . they might have gone by now, I guess. It's probably nothing.'

I marvelled at my brother again. If there was one thing guaranteed to get Nicky's interest it was the phrase, 'It's probably nothing.'

Nicky hesitated. 'We've had trouble with graffiti lately. The town council is up in arms about it. I could have a quick look, I suppose. Just to make sure.' She swung back to face us. 'You two will stay on the main road, yes? Just down into town and then back again? Don't go wandering off anywhere—and stay away from that phone mast on the hill, OK? I know you like it up there, Holly, but that mast is dangerous.'

'Oh, I know,' I said, thinking of the lightning strike. Joe trod on my foot.

'Right, well, I expect I'll catch up with you later,' Nicky said, already starting to walk away. 'Give your mum my love. I'll pop in on her this evening, see how she is.'

'OK!' I waved at her. Then I turned to my brother. 'You were amazing!'

'Yeah? You were **RUBBISH**.' He gave me a stern look. 'You *know* the mast is dangerous? Don't say stuff like that to her!'

'Sorry. I knew as soon as I spoke . . . '

He huffed, and we headed back down the road into town. Past the supermarket, the fabric shop, the shoe shop, the 'tat' shops (the ones that sell flippers and flip-flops and baskets and beach balls) and the leather glove shop. Yes—we have a shop that sells *only* leather gloves. Crazy.

We managed to avoid having to talk to

anyone else along the way, though we did have to wave at several people who knew us. That's the trouble with a small place where everyone knows everyone else. I kept my eye out for clues, but I didn't see anything unusual.

Unlike Joe, who kept saying, 'See that bump in the brickwork of this wall? It's new, isn't it? Maybe someone bundled Imogen into the back of a van and in their hurry to get away they drove into the wall?' Or, 'Since when did Classic Cards close? It's all boarded up. Do you think Imogen could be being held in there?'

In the end, I stopped and said, 'This isn't a *game*, Joe.'

He looked hurt. 'Of course it isn't. But how are you ever going to solve a mystery without imagination? I'm just coming up with ideas. I'm not saying they're *right*.'

I wished I had imagination. I just couldn't think of *anything* that might have happened to Imogen. Everything just seemed impossible. Which meant that, if you went by my reasoning, she'd still be in the last place anyone saw her. **WHICH WAS** . . .

My steps slowed to a halt outside the bakery. 'Joe . . . ' I said. **'What if she's still at CyberSky?'**

CHAPTER 15

He stared at me, shoving his hands into his pockets. 'But Professor Macavity said . . . ' Then he stopped, pulling out the white stringy wormy thing we'd found in my mobile. We both looked at it. 'What if there's a bigger mystery here?' he said. 'What if Imogen found out something about the CyberSky phones?'

'Something really bad?' I asked.

'They wouldn't want her to tell anyone,' he went on. 'So they'd have to make sure she couldn't . . . '

I felt a **WAVE OF FEAR** wash over me. 'Do you think . . . she's **DEAD**?'

His face was pale. 'I don't know. Surely not?'

'It happens in comics,' I whispered.

'But this is real life,' he whispered back. 'Isn't it? I mean . . . '

My fingers tingled, and I pressed my hands

together. 'We were going to walk down there anyway, weren't we?'

He swallowed and nodded. 'All right. Just to take a look.'

My legs felt wobbly as we set off again, and my fingers kept prickling. I rubbed them irritably. They felt like they'd been stung by nettles. I had half a mind to suggest to Joe that we turn round and go home, but I dismissed it as silly. We were only going to LOOK at the CyberSky building, weren't we? We could go home at ANY TIME . . .

The further out of town we went and the closer to the CyberSky building, the worse the prickling in my fingers got. And then it started in my chest too, and I could feel all the tiny hairs on the back of my neck standing up. 'Joe,' I said, trying to sound calm, 'something weird's happening to me.'

He looked sharply at me. 'What kind of weird?'

'Look.' I held up my hands. Tiny SPARKS were jumping off my fingertips.

Joe took a step away from me so as to avoid an accidental shock. 'Whoa. Are you doing that on purpose?'

'No, of course not! It's just happening!'

He frowned and looked up and down the road. On the far side, the ground stretched out in parkland for a hundred metres or so before dropping sharply down to rocks and the sea. Ahead of us, the grey tarmac snaked along the coast before climbing steeply into the hills. Back the way we had come, the road was soon invisible, squashed between the shops and businesses. It was a nice day—hot, but the breeze took the edge off the sun. Gulls circled and cried; a boat snailed slowly across the bay.

To our left, sitting squatly at the base of the hill, was the mirrored building, reflecting the blue of the sky in the smoky greyness of its windows.

There were only four people in sight: a couple standing on our side of the road up ahead, looking out over the sea with binoculars; a man coming along the road behind us, walking a very big dog which was straining at the lead; and a teenage girl sitting on a bench in the park opposite, looking down at the phone in her hands.

Joe edged a little closer to me and said in a low voice, 'Are you about to *blow something up?*'

'I don't think so,' I whispered back. 'It's more like … there's lots of ELECTRICITY already here. It's not coming from me. I mean, I'm not making it. It's *here*, somehow. Under the ground, maybe?'

We both stared at the pavement. 'Under the ground?' murmured Joe. 'But what could be down there except rock?'

I opened my mouth to reply, but instead I said, 'OOF!' as something really huge shoved me from behind, knocking me over.

'Sorry, love!' It was the man with the enormous dog. He pulled on the lead and the dog—a big, black, bouncy thing with a pink tongue—jerked back, fidgeting and snuffling. 'Are you OK?'

I rubbed my elbow. 'Yeah, I'm OK.' The dog was even bigger from this angle! It was excitedly sniffing the air and trying to lick me. 'Wow, it's—uh—friendly.'

'Oh, Thor wouldn't hurt a fly,' said the man fondly. He had round glasses and a beanie hat that mostly covered his shock of black hair, along with a dark green anorak that had seen better days. 'He looks fierce but he doesn't even bark at the postman.'

'Can I stroke him?' asked Joe, whose eyes had

lit up. He's always wanted a dog.

'Course you can,' said the man, beaming. 'He loves kids.'

Joe stroked Thor enthusiastically, and Thor tried to lick his face.

'Go on,' the man said to me. 'You can too, if you like.'

I stretched out a hand to Thor—a hand tingling with electricity . . .

HOLLY REACHED FOR THE DOG, BUT SHE'D FORGOTTEN HOW MUCH ELECTRICITY WAS AROUND!

YELP!

I pulled my hand back quickly. 'I'm so sorry! I—I don't know what happened.'

The man crouched down to cuddle the dog, which was whimpering. 'That was some burst of static!' he said in an astonished voice. 'You been rubbing balloons on your head or something?'

'Uh, no . . . ' I said. Joe swung round to glare at me. 'I mean, yeah . . . ' I corrected myself. 'And bouncing on our trampoline. I always get static off that. Sorry. Is Thor OK?'

'He'll be fine,' said the man, straightening up again. 'Funny, though. I've had a couple of electric shocks myself around here recently. Wondered if it was something to do with that new building.' He nodded towards the grey smoky windows of CyberSky. 'I even went up to ask 'em. I said, "You got a jumbo-sized generator in there or something?"'

'What did they say?' asked Joe.

The man shrugged. 'Told me to go away. They said, "We know all about you, Steve Sloane. Always poking your nose in where it doesn't belong."' He gave us a hurt look. 'I was just asking what any normal person would ask! But they're **NOT NORMAL**, are they, the people in there?'

'Aren't they?' I asked, curious. 'What do you mean?'

Steve shrugged. At his feet, Thor sat obediently, as still as a statue. 'Got this **weird look in their eyes,** haven't they? Like they're not properly there. Lights are on but nobody's home, you know? Maybe it saps the brain, working here. Maybe all this talk about radiation is right, after all.'

I rolled my eyes. 'That's what my mum says.'

'You don't believe her, huh?' Steve glanced around and lowered his voice. 'I've seen lights in the sky round here—not planes, they're too fast. Didn't happen before these people came. Don't tell *me* they're not using **ALIEN TECHNOLOGY.**'

I caught Joe's gaze and tried not to snigger. CyberSky making UFOs?! The sooner we got away from this crazy guy, the better.

'You're young,' Steve said, noticing my expression. 'When you've lived as long as I have, you'll know. There are things that can't be explained by science. Powers beyond our understanding.' He nodded towards CyberSky. 'That place—it's bad. I feel it in my bones. You stay away from it. And from those phones.' Then he looked down. 'Ahh *no*, Thor. Not on the *pavement*.'

Joe and I began to sidle away while Steve picked up a huge dog poo with a bag. Thor gave a bark of enthusiasm and wagged his tail. 'Well,' I said vaguely, 'nice to meet you.'

'You stay away from that place,' Steve said, tying the bag in a knot. 'I tell you, there's something wrong about it. And what do they need all this electricity for anyway? You'd think they were creating Frankenstein's monster!' He gave a great laugh.

We watched him set off with his dog, crossing the road to the grassy area, where Steve unclipped Thor's lead. The black dog took off across the grass like a rocket and before long they were both out of sight.

'What a nutter,' said Joe at last.

I grinned. 'Says you! The boy who reads comics and believes them!'

He raised his eyebrows at me. 'Says the girl with **ELECTRIC SUPERPOWERS**.'

'Yeah, all right,' I said. 'Fair point. But he *is* off his rocker.'

'I dunno.' Joe glanced up at the huge mirrored windows. 'He said there was something wrong about this place . . . '

I stared up at it, my fingers crackling with

power more than ever. 'I do feel weird. Like superpower-weird.'

'Spidey-senses,' said Joe solemnly.

'Whatever. What do we do now?'

He looked at me, astonished. '*We go in, of course.* What did you think we were going to do?'

CHAPTER 16

Before I could stop him, Joe had marched right up to the grey, shiny, *forbidding* front door and knocked on it. 'Hello? Anybody in there?'

'*Joe,*' I whispered fiercely. 'What are you *doing?*'

There was a pause and then a security guard opened the front door. He was a really big man. Even taller than Dad. And he was wearing a grey uniform with the CyberSky logo on his sleeve. 'What do you want?' he asked, frowning.

'Hi,' said Joe, putting on his most innocent childlike smile. 'I was here yesterday? With the group who were on a special visit?'

'Yes?' said the guard, though his voice sounded a little less hostile.

'I left my pencil case here,' said Joe. 'By mistake. Upstairs, in the room with all the . . . gadgets.'

The guard's eyes narrowed slightly. 'Yeah?'

'Yeah. And I wouldn't bother you only it's my best pencil case and it's got this special pen in it.' Joe let his voice wobble. 'My dad bought me the pen before he went off on his latest assignment. He's in the army, you see . . . '

I have to admit, I **WAS IMPRESSED**. All that making his own films had obviously paid off when it came to Joe's acting ability. Even his eyes looked full of unshed tears!

The guard was obviously impressed too. 'Sorry, son,' he said gruffly. 'I'd like to let you in but it's more than my job's worth. If you come back tomorrow, I'll tell you if we've found it.'

'But I need it tonight!' Joe's voice actually **CRACKED**. Even though I knew he was faking, I felt really upset for him! 'I've got to write an essay for school about my dad and what he means to me—and I have to do it with that pen! I *have* to!'

It would have melted a heart of stone. I was practically in tears myself. And for a moment, I thought that maybe it had worked. The guard threw me a pleading look. 'Is this your brother?' he asked, in a husky tone.

'Yes,' I said, grateful that I didn't have to lie.

The guard swallowed. 'Quite a trooper, isn't he?' He ruffled Joe's hair, and I pressed my lips together to prevent a giggle because I know Joe **HATES** it when anyone does that. 'I'd be proud to have a son like you,' he told Joe. 'And I wish I could help, I really do. But I'd lose my job in an instant.'

'Oh,' said Joe in a very small, defeated voice. 'Oh. Oh well. Sorry to have bothered you.' He turned to me and said, 'Dad will understand, won't he?'

'Of course he will,' I said. 'It's OK. We'll find you another pen. I know it won't be as good . . . '

'Wait!' the guard interrupted. He was wiping his eye. 'Look, I can't let you in. But I can go and have a look for you, OK? What does it look like, this pencil case?'

'Uh . . . ' said Joe, rubbing his own eyes and clearing his throat. I knew he was just playing for time to think up a good answer. 'It's a Spider-Man one.'

'From the comics or the films?' asked the guard.

Joe looked outraged. 'The comics, of course.'

The guard smiled. His whole face lit up, and suddenly I thought maybe he was a really nice person underneath the grumpy-guardness. 'Good lad. Excellent taste. I'll go and check through the rooms you were in yesterday. Give me ten minutes, OK?'

'OK,' said Joe, beaming back.

'What's your name?' asked the guard.

'Joe.'

'Hi, Joe, I'm Kelvin.' They shook hands seriously. Kelvin glanced at me.

'This is my sister Holly,' Joe said.

Kelvin held out his hand to me, and I SO nearly took it. But then I remembered I'd given Thor the dog an **ELECTRIC SHOCK!!** I couldn't risk the same thing happening here! So I gave Kelvin an embarrassed wave instead and then jammed my hands into my pockets again, squeezing them into fists in an effort to control the tingling.

Kelvin looked slightly surprised, but then he shrugged and grinned at Joe. 'Right,' he said. 'See you in ten.' He ruffled Joe's hair again, and went back into the building. The door swung to a close behind him . . .

. . . right onto Joe's foot.

CHAPTER 17

'You were **AWESOME**,' I told my brother, and I meant it.

'Yeah, I know,' he said completely un-modestly. 'Come on, this is our chance.'

We peeked through the gap in the not-quite-closed door but there was no sign of Kelvin the friendly guard, so we pushed the door all the way open and went in. My fingers practically **HURT** with all the electricity **SPARKING** between them, and I rubbed my aching chest, taking a quick peek to see if the burn pattern had appeared. Thankfully it hadn't, but I had this horrible feeling it might appear soon.

The foyer of CyberSky was big and airy, with a high ceiling stretching up to more smoky grey glass, and a big grey desk in the middle of the shiny grey floor. Actually, just assume from now on that everything I describe in the building is grey, because really, that's how it was. Grey walls, grey desk, grey computer monitor on the guard's desk, grey telephone . . . it's kind of boring to repeat, so I won't bother. But just remember—everything's grey, OK?

'Whoa,' said Joe, looking around. 'That's a lot of grey.'

We are SO over the grey.

The reception desk looked like a rectangular island in the middle of this shiny sea. To our far right and left were doors—all closed, of course. Joe and I walked cautiously around the desk. Behind the two chairs was more shiny floor, and right at the back of the airy atrium were double doors that anyone would recognize.

'Lifts,' I said to Joe, pointing.

He grinned. 'Where shall we go? Up or down?'

I stretched out my hands. Sparks jumped between my fingers. 'There's so much power here! I'm sure it's coming from underneath us.'

'Down, then,' said Joe, nodding in agreement. 'Before the guard comes back.'

I pressed the button for the lift, pulling my finger back with an exclamation as I accidentally created a spark with the metal. 'I mustn't touch anything! This is *really* dangerous!'

The doors slid open with a whisper. 'I'd better press this one then,' said Joe, looking at the panel of numbers and letters. '*Going DOWN . . .*'

He pressed the button right at the bottom: the one simply marked 'Z'. The doors slid shut and the lift started to descend. And as it did . . .

HOLLY AND JOE DIDN'T KNOW IT BUT THEY WERE BEING OBSERVED ...

Focus, Holly! BREATHE ...

REC

AS HOLLY REGAINED CONTROL, THE BURN PATTERN DISAPPEARED AND SHE WAS NO LONGER A THREAT ... FOR NOW!

I opened my eyes. Joe was grinning at me. 'That's good,' he said. 'Well done.'

Then the lift doors whooshed open, and my heart sped up again. But it was OK, because as one quick glance showed, there were no angry security guards on the other side, ready to throw us in dungeons. In fact, the space outside the lift was very small indeed, no bigger than our porch at home. The straight grey walls extended maybe two metres in front of us and ended in a big grey door. Which was shut, of course.

We stepped out of the lift and Joe examined the door. 'Electronic keypad,' he said in some satisfaction, and turned to look at me.

My heart was thumping really hard. 'Maybe we should go back. I mean, we don't know the code. And we don't even know that Imogen is down here. We could get in *real* trouble.'

'We can't go back,' Joe said. 'Something's going on. And you said yourself this is the most likely place she'd be. Even if she isn't, don't you *want* to know what this is all about? Why they've got white worms in the phones? Why this place is crawling with electricity? Come ON, Holly! This is the **BIGGEST ADVENTURE EVER!**'

'It's not safe,' I said. 'It's specially not safe for you. You might get hurt. What would I tell Mum? I mean, you're right: I do want to know what's going on. And if Imogen's here, I want to find her. But you should go back.'

Joe's face darkened like thunder. '**NO WAY!**' he shouted at me. 'No way are you leaving me out of this! This is MY thing! All my life I've been waiting for a REAL comic strip to happen to me, and now here it is, and you think I should go HOME?! You are JOKING!'

I looked down, feeling like I'd been told off. 'All right,' I said sulkily. 'But it doesn't make any difference. We still can't get through the door.'

Joe rolled his eyes. 'Er, hello? Superpowers?!'

'Oh! Well, yeah, but I've just switched them off!'

'Well, switch them on again!' said Joe, exasperated. 'Honestly, why did it have to be YOU? I'd have made a WAY better superhero!'

'All RIGHT, all right!' It took only a few seconds for me to summon my powers . . .

HOLLY PLACED HER HAND ON THE KEYPAD . . .

I closed my eyes and concentrated on my breathing to switch off my powers again. It worked! I opened my eyes and smiled smugly. '*Hah!*'

'*Finally*,' muttered Joe. 'It's like going on an adventure with Clark Kent instead of Superman.'

'Oh, stop moaning,' I said, pushing on the door. 'I thought you *wanted* to see Frankenstein's monster?' Grinning at my brother, I stepped through the doorway . . .

And straight into the path of Professor Macavity.

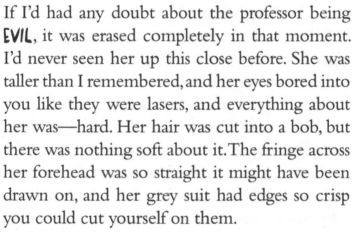

CHAPTER 18

If I'd had any doubt about the professor being **EVIL**, it was erased completely in that moment. I'd never seen her up this close before. She was taller than I remembered, and her eyes bored into you like they were lasers, and everything about her was—hard. Her hair was cut into a bob, but there was nothing soft about it. The fringe across her forehead was so straight it might have been drawn on, and her grey suit had edges so crisp you could cut yourself on them.

She was looking at me as though I were something that had *crawled out from under a rock*. I felt myself shrink. Superpowers? What use would they be against someone like her? She could shrivel me with one look! I had been the biggest fool ever to come here. Behind me, Joe gave a kind of strangled gasp.

The professor was flanked by two security

guards, dressed in the same uniform as Kelvin had been upstairs. The room wasn't very big but it was obviously some kind of surveillance centre because on either side of us there were loads of TV screens, showing the CyberSky building from inside and out. I realized we must have been spotted from the moment we talked to Kelvin, and my heart sank. What chance did we have against all this?

'This is very interesting,' said Professor Macavity, her arms folded. Her voice had almost no inflection; it was like she was speaking through a machine. 'And who are you?'

I swallowed. My mouth had dried up completely. 'Holly Sparkes,' I managed to croak.

'Holly Sparkes,' she repeated, and her eyes narrowed. 'Why are you here?'

I couldn't even think of a lie. Her gaze was worse than Mrs Lester's, worse than the strictest teacher you can imagine. It made my brain turn to mush. 'I'm—I'm looking for my friend,' I stuttered. 'Imogen Clump.'

One sharp eyebrow jolted upwards into a triangle. 'The missing girl? What makes you think she's here?'

'Er . . . ' I said. But my brain had stopped

supplying even the truth. I just stared, struck dumb.

'Because of *this*.' My brother stepped forward. In his hand he held out my busted phone, the white stringy stuff trailing over his fingers. 'We know *exactly* what you're up to.'

I nearly fainted. What was Joe *doing*? We would never get out of here alive! Mum would never know what had happened to us . . . and neither would Dad . . . I felt sick and cold with fear.

But the effect on the professor was astonishing. Her mouth dropped open, and for the first time she looked taken aback. 'What—how did you . . . ?' Then the mask hardened on her face again and her lips thinned to pencil lines. 'I see. Perhaps we should have a talk. Somewhere secure.'

Secure?! I knew what THAT meant! Secure meant LOCKED! My head began to spin, and my fingers to tingle. I forgot all about my breathing. She was going to lock us up, and we'd never go home again!

I BEGAN TO PANIC . . .

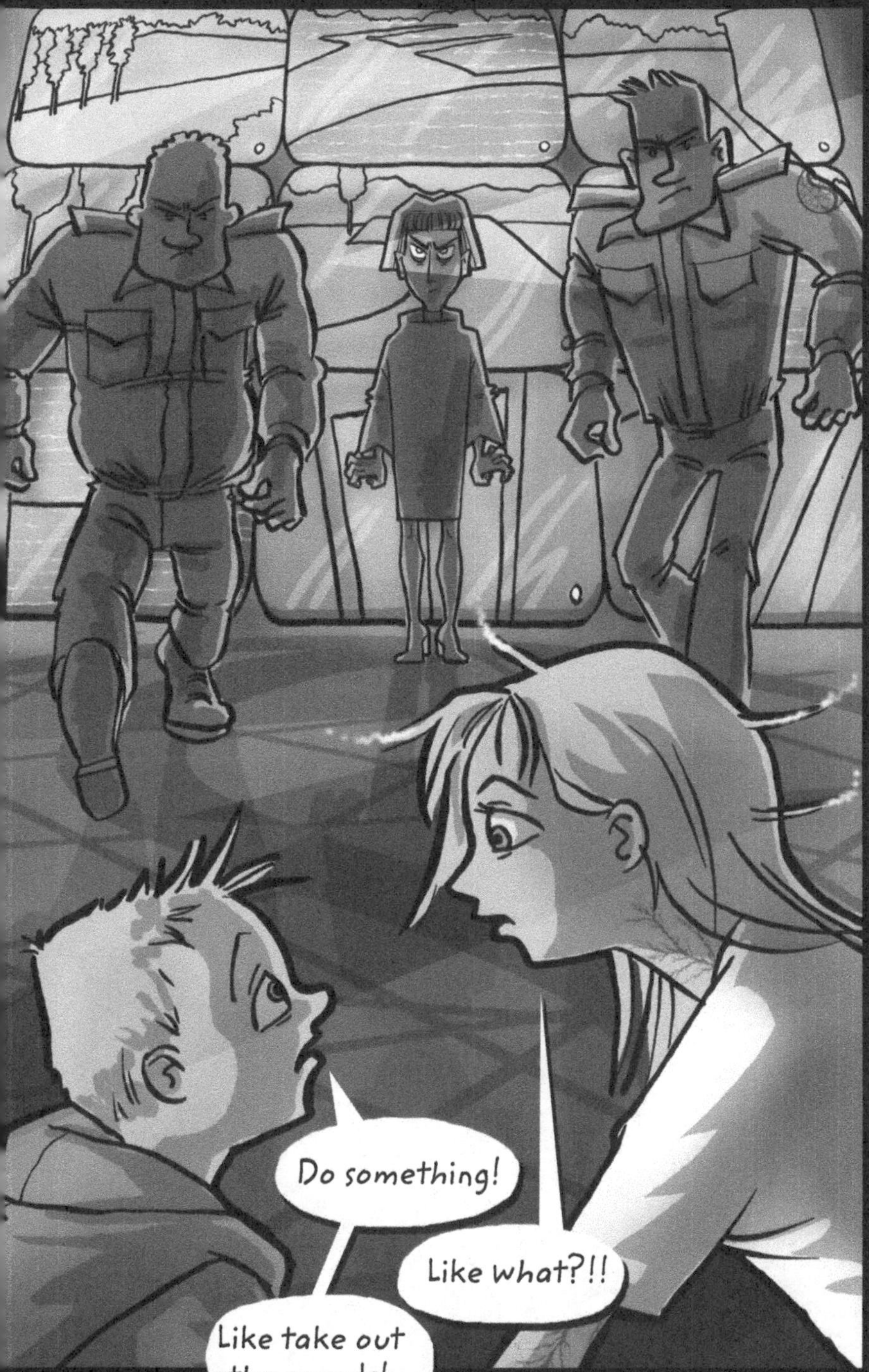
Do something!
Like what?!!
Like take out the guards!

THE SECURITY GUARDS WERE DOWN—
BUT WHERE WAS PROFESSOR MACAVITY?

I felt suddenly tired and dizzy, and I knew my powers had vanished again. I'd never unleashed that amount of electricity before—and I hadn't meant to either! Those poor guards!

'Don't check them!' Joe blurted, as I bent down to Kelvin. 'In films, they always come back to life just as you're making sure they're dead!'

'I'm making sure they're **ALIVE**!' I exclaimed. 'This isn't a film, Joe, these are real people!' My trembling fingers felt for a pulse in Kelvin's neck. Dad had shown me how to find a pulse years ago. 'You never know when it might come in handy,' he'd said.

To my HUGE relief, Kelvin's heart was still beating. Thank goodness—he was still alive! Quickly, I checked the other two, trying to ignore the lethargy in my arms and legs. Using superpowers *really* took it out of me. But at least I wasn't about to hurt anyone else, and the other two guards were also still alive. 'I must have knocked them out with electricity,' I said in wonder. 'I didn't even know you could do that.'

'Of course you can,' Joe said, as if I were stupid. 'Like lightning, or an electric shock from a plug.

Your body runs on electricity—everyone's does. We generate low levels of the stuff all the time. Like synapses firing in the brain. And in your heart too—that's why you can give someone an electric shock to save them when they've had a heart attack.'

'You've been reading up,' I commented.

'That's what mentors do,' he informed me smugly.

'How long do you think we have before they wake up?' I asked.

He shrugged. 'Best not hang around to find out. There are bound to be more guards on the way. And besides, we haven't found Imogen yet.'

'That's true.' I got to my feet. 'Well, there's only one way to go, isn't there?'

We both looked at the door Professor Macavity had used. 'It's that or back to the lift,' agreed Joe. 'You ready?'

I clenched my fists. I'd just taken out three guards. I'd fought the baddies! So what if using my powers made me tired? A bit of yawning wasn't going to stop me rescuing my best friend! Bring on Frankenstein's monster!

'Let's go,' I said.

CHAPTER 19

My secret was out now. There was no point trying to sneak around any more. Professor Macavity knew we were here, and she knew what I could do. The only option we had was to walk into her lair and hope we were strong enough to win.

I was REALLY glad my brother was with me.

Though OBVIOUSLY I'd never tell him that.

I put out a hand to open the door, but Joe said, 'Wait a minute. I think you should go in alone. *Like a proper superhero.*'

'What?' My voice shook a bit. 'Aren't you coming with me?'

'Of course I am—but not right beside you. You need me hidden elsewhere, so that I can help when I need to. You're the one she's interested in—the one with the powers. If you go in as strong as you can, I'll slip out to one side. Then I can go look for Imogen while you keep her talking. OK?'

'Keep her *talking?* Joe, I don't really do talking, not like you . . .'

'Blow something up then,' he said. 'But don't get us killed, OK?'

'Oh. OK.' I felt a bit better. I knew how to blow things up! 'Right, then. Ready?'

'Ready.'

I reached out to the door again, summoning my powers. What would I have to face on the other side? As the door slowly opened, I could hardly believe what I was seeing . . .

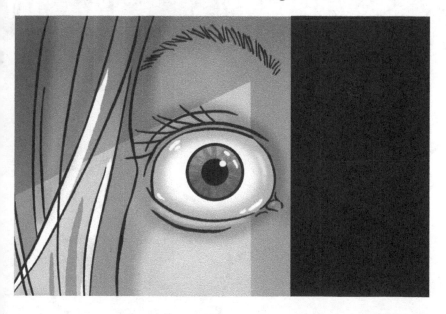

HOLLY HAD DISCOVERED THE HEART OF CYBERSKY!

AND THEN SOMETHING HAPPENED THAT NO ONE EXPECTED . . .
FSHMMMMM
My Machine! It's . . . it's CONNECTING with her!!
THE METAL MACHINE, THAT MONSTROUS BEAST, WAS PART ALIVE!

Switch it off!
CLUNK!
WHMMMMM
I can hardly move . . . so tired . . .
That's more electrical power than I've ever seen . . . and the girl is still alive! But HOW?

I lay on the floor, feeling like I'd been hit by a ten-ton truck. What on earth had just happened? I could barely lift my arms, and my head hummed as though filled with invisible bees. *That Machine! What WAS it?* For a few moments, I had felt more alive than ever before. Power had surged through me—I could have done anything! But now I felt totally drained, like the Machine had sucked all my powers out of me. Was that what it was doing to Imogen?

I lay on the floor, hardly able to lift my head. I heard the professor say from a long way off, 'These readings can't be right. Are you sure this is functioning correctly? The Machine has never generated this amount of power before!'

What *was* she on about? I wished my head wasn't so fuzzy because I wanted to think. Where was Joe? I hoped he was safe.

Then footsteps came towards me, and the professor's voice came from a lot closer. 'Holly Sparkes,' she said. 'Sparkes by name, Sparkes by nature, it seems. What *are* you, exactly?'

What are you? I didn't know how to answer. My brain couldn't think.

She took a step closer. I could see her grey court shoes, with their small heel and shiny patent leather. 'By rights you should be dead. No human can survive that level of electricity. So *what are you?*'

'I'm . . . I'm a girl,' I croaked. '*Just a girl.*'

She made a sound I didn't recognize for a moment. And then I realized. She was *laughing*. Was the world going utterly insane?! '*Just* a girl,' she repeated. 'Oh, I don't think so. You, Miss Sparkes, are an electric phenomenon. AN ELECTRIC GIRL.' Her voice dropped to a sinister whisper, cold as fog in a graveyard. 'Tell me, Holly. Have you always been like this, or did something happen to you?'

I was so tired! I couldn't even begin to tell her the story—not that I wanted to, anyway. And besides, at the back of my fuzzy mind, I had the strongest feeling that there was something I was here to do . . . someone I was here to find . . .

'Imogen!' I gasped, and my head cleared in an instant. I was here to rescue Imogen! I struggled to my feet, swaying unsteadily on my shaky legs. '*You,*' I said to the professor, who had taken a step back, 'you let my friend go. I'm not telling you *anything.*'

She raised both eyebrows at me. 'Oh really?'

I looked past her, at my bestest best friend

ever, slumped in the chair in the middle of that horrible machine. 'Imogen!' I called. 'Imogen, can you hear me?' But Imogen didn't move. '*If you've killed her,*' I said to the professor, and anger flooded through me, erasing the exhaustion. 'If she's dead . . . '

'Don't be hysterical,' snapped the professor. 'If there's one thing I can't stand it's a child having a tantrum. Of course she's not dead; she's part of the Machine.

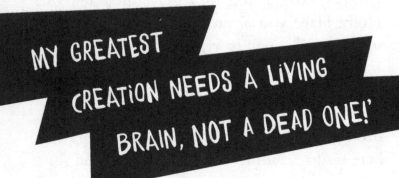

MY GREATEST CREATION NEEDS A LIVING BRAIN, NOT A DEAD ONE!'

CHAPTER 20

I stared at her. 'A living brain?' Something in me went EWWWWWW and another part of me went EEEEEEKK! A metal machine using a human brain! It was like a horror film! 'But why?' I asked, trying not to gag. 'What's it for?'

'You're a child,' said the professor. 'You wouldn't understand. This is highly developed technology.'

'Don't patronize me,' I said crossly. 'My generation has grown up with technology. We even learn programming at school. This isn't technology. This is using real stuff inside machines. Like your phones. That white stringy yuck . . .'

Professor Macavity gave a cold smile. 'It's derived from JELLYFISH. It carries electrical signals faster and more efficiently than fibreoptic wires. And it can generate its own electrical waves too, on the same frequency as a brain.'

There she was again, going on about brains! 'I think you must have *brains on the brain*,' I said, wishing that Joe were beside me to hear me crack a witty joke in such a stressful situation.

'My background is in neuroscience,' said the professor. 'The human brain is the most fascinating thing on this planet. Over half of it is never used. If part of it is destroyed, it can transfer the skills located in that section to a different one. It grows new synaptic links all the time, especially . . . ' her smile grew wider, until it was **TRULY SCARY**, 'in *children*.' Then she turned to look at Imogen.

I felt faint. 'You've done something to Imogen's brain,' I breathed.

'Her phone did,' the professor said. 'All that time she was doing the quizzes, the jellyfish string was responding to her brainwaves, altering them and sending them back to her. Her brain is perfect for my needs.'

'What needs?' I asked. 'You're not going to tell me you want **WORLD DOMINATION**. That's SO last century.'

The smile vanished. 'You foolish child. You think world domination involves invading countries, overthrowing leaders, guns and ships and war? The whole world is online. One only needs access to critical areas. Highly secure sites, intelligence organizations, email systems within governments. Not to mention grass-roots areas like food supply. Why, with one short sequence sent from here, all meat supply could be halted. Or bread. Or soap. Or . . . water. Electricity. How long do you think it takes before people turn on each other? They say civilization is only two meals away from savagery.'

'*You're mad*,' I said, staring. 'Bonkers. Barking. Totally insane.'

'How much do you think people will pay for my technology?' Macavity was grinning again. 'With this Machine, I can control *everything*. And your little friend has been helping to set it all up.'

'What? How?'

'Her brain . . . ' Macavity tapped the side of her head. 'We simply run information through her brain, and use her creativity to make leaps of ingenuity and imagination. Do you know who make the best code-breakers? Children. Because they have more imagination than adults. Imogen's brain has been helping the

Machine to develop the most sophisticated code-breaking programs the world has ever seen!'

'That's not fair!' I exclaimed. 'It's not your brain, it's hers! She would **NEVER** help you do something so totally sick!'

'Whereas *your* brain . . . ' The professor's voice altered. Her head tilted very slightly to one side as she looked at me. 'Your brain appears to be capable of generating very high voltage without any damage to your body. Extraordinary. You are, in effect, a **HUMAN BATTERY.**'

'*Yeah*,' I said, feeling that now was the time to make some kind of stand. 'Yeah, I am. I could blow up everything in this room. And I *will*—if you don't let my friend go.'

There was a very long pause. I held my breath as Macavity and I looked at each other. Now was the moment. I had made my demand. Who would blink first?

Then the professor opened her mouth and said,

'GET THE GiRL OUT OF THE MACHiNE.'

Elation flooded through me. I had won! I had done it! Professor Macavity was backing down!

I felt like a *real* superhero. **AWESOME**.

In the middle of the Machine, a technician was undoing the straps that held Imogen in her seat. Finally, he lifted the helmet from her head. As it came away, Imogen's eyes opened and she stared around blurrily. 'My head . . . ' she said in a tired voice.

'Imogen!' I ran to her. 'Imogen, it's me!'

Imogen looked at me. Her eyes seemed unfocused. 'Holly . . . ?'

I took her arm; squeezed her hand. 'I'm right here. You're going to be OK.'

She got up out of the chair, rubbing her head. 'Where am I?'

'At CyberSky,' I said, grinning all over my face. 'You never left. But don't worry. We're going home.'

'Oh, I don't think so,' came the cold grey tones of Professor Macavity.

I whipped around. 'What? You said . . . but you're letting Imogen go! Right?'

Her shoulders lifted very slightly in an almost imperceptible shrug. 'Perhaps. She's of little interest to me now.'

'But then . . . ' I trailed off. Two technicians were closing in on us. A sudden dread gripped me. 'What—what are you doing?'

'**Plug in the other one,**' the professor said to the technicians. 'But do it fast before she can use her power.'

'What—no!' The technicians shoved Imogen out of the way, and pushed me down into the seat she had just left. I was so taken aback, I didn't have time to resist—and before I knew it, the straps were being tightened across my arms and legs.

I froze. You know that stupid thing when you *know* you should fight or scream or do SOMETHING but you can't because you're too SCARED? Well—that. My brain couldn't think. I just went *EEEE*KKK! inside my own head, and nothing worked.

'What's going on? What are you doing to her?' I heard Imogen say in a weak voice.

'Not the same thing we did to you,' the professor replied. 'Your friend is capable of generating high levels of electricity—higher, possibly, than we can generate ourselves. And if there's one thing this Machine needs, it's power—lots and lots of power.'

'You—you're mad!' Imogen cried. 'Holly's just a girl!'

'No,' said the professor, 'she's very much more than that. And this Machine can use her. With the code-breaking programs in place, everything is ready to go; and your little friend can ensure that this Machine works faster than it could ever have done by itself. She's a human electric power source.'

I was trembling. Even using my powers myself left me weak and exhausted. If the Machine used me, there would be nothing left of me! Could you die from exhaustion? Joe had said hearts contained electricity . . . would mine simply give up the struggle?

A tiny flicker inside my head said . . . *where's Joe?*

But it was too late to worry about him. I lifted my head, now tightly encased in the metal helmet, to see Professor Macavity nod to one of the technicians. Imogen, white as a ghost, was being held back by a security guard—one of the ones I'd blasted earlier. I gazed helplessly at my best friend. 'I'm so sorry,' I said.

Imogen burst into tears. 'I'm sorry too! All that time—it was like I was someone else! I didn't care about anything except those stupid quizzes! And I was so horrible to you! I'll make it up to you, Holly, I promise!'

But you won't get the chance, I thought. It's too late. Neither of us will ever leave here again . . .

AND THEN I SAW THE TECHNICIAN
PULL DOWN THE LEVER
TO SWITCH ON
THE MACHINE . . .

FROM HIS HIDING PLACE, JOE WATCHED HELPLESSLY.
Professor! The levels are rising too fast! Are you sure this is safe?
WHMMMMMM!!!
Don't touch that lever! Can't you see how the Machine is feeding off her power?
She can't win against that! But what can I do?

BUT IMOGEN DIDN'T GIVE UP THAT EASILY!
Fight, Holly! You can do it. I know you can. You're my BEST FRIEND!
FIGHTTTTT
She's still my best friend! I MUST FIGHT!
Professor, the levels! She'll break it apart!

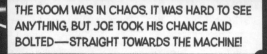

THE ROOM WAS IN CHAOS. IT WAS HARD TO SEE ANYTHING, BUT JOE TOOK HIS CHANCE AND BOLTED—STRAIGHT TOWARDS THE MACHINE!

BOOM!

IMOGEN'S GUARDS TURNED AND RAN

I didn't sign up for this! I'm outta here!

Holly, **STOP!!!** Everything is **EXPLODING!**

FINALLY THE THREE HEROES STAGGERED OUT INTO THE BLINDING SUNLIGHT . . .

CHAPTER 22

My head hurt terribly, and it was hard to see. I heard Imogen shouting, 'Over here! Help, someone!' and then start coughing. Joe, on my other side, was coughing too. Smoke billowed out from the building behind us. I couldn't remember getting into the lift at all—how had it still been working? And was the whole building about to fall down? 'We should get away . . .' I mumbled, but no one heard me.

Minutes later, or it could have been hours, I wasn't sure, I was in the back of an ambulance. A machine was beeping, and I felt sticky pads on my neck and chest. Something cool was pressed to my face, and I heard a woman murmuring about burn marks. I could also hear Joe chattering loudly, saying something about a **MALFUNCTION** and me receiving an **ELECTRIC SHOCK**. He was talking far more loudly than he needed to, and then I realized he was trying to give me a message. *Don't say anything about what really happened! They're doctors; they'll want to examine your brain and find out about your powers!*

I tried to sit up, to tell Joe that I'd heard, but the paramedic pushed me down again and said gently, 'No, you rest now. We'll take care of everything.'

I lay back and stared tiredly at the sunlight on the ceiling of the ambulance. My head felt so fuzzy! And the skin on my face was so sore. There was no trace of electricity around my hands now. I wondered if the Machine had drained my powers completely. Would I go back to being ordinary Holly Sparkes again? Somehow, the thought made me *really* sad.

Then a shadow passed over the ceiling, and I heard a deep voice from outside. 'Hi, folks. We're going to take it from here, thanks.'

The paramedic by my side got up and went to the back. There was a short confused conversation, and then Imogen came up to my head. 'Holly,' she said, puzzled, 'there's a man here who says you can go home. I don't know who he is. It's all kind of . . . odd.'

I sat up, rubbing my head. 'Odd? What man?' Then I glanced out of the doors and gasped in surprise.

Steve Sloane, the dog walker, was looking in at me. But something about him was different. He looked taller, somehow—more businesslike—and he'd taken off his glasses. He nodded at me. 'Good work, Holly.'

My eyes opened wide. I thought he was a crazy alien-obsessed dog-walker, but he was talking like someone in charge! Did he know what had happened inside? 'Er . . . ' I said.

'Don't worry,' he cut across me. 'We're taking care of everything. You can go home. I've rung your mother and she's coming to pick up you and your brother. Imogen's parents are on their way too.'

'But . . . ' I said, utterly baffled. 'Aren't I going to the hospital?'

His eyes, brown and direct, met mine. 'Do you want to?'

'N-no,' I said. 'Not really.'

He smiled. 'I told you not to go in, you and your brother. Should have known you wouldn't listen. But I never knew Imogen was in there—I'd have taken action sooner if I had.'

I rubbed my head. 'I don't understand . . . '

'Don't worry,' he said. 'Everything's going to be fine. Your secret's safe with me. I have a lot of secrets.'

'You don't say,' I replied, wondering if everyone was completely mad around here.

Steve gave me a nod. 'I'll be in touch.'

'Wait!' I said as he turned to go. 'What about the PROFESSOR? Is she still down there?'

'She hasn't come out. But we've got all the exits covered.' He hesitated. 'She may not be alive, of course. That was a pretty big EXPLOSION.'

'Mmm,' I said, suddenly feeling a bit guilty.

He gave me another smile. 'You're something special, Holly Sparkes. We'll be watching out for you, to make sure you're safe.'

'We who?' I asked, but he'd gone. I blinked. 'This is turning out to be the weirdest day of my life EVER. And where's his dog?'

'What dog?' Imogen took my hand. 'Holly, are you sure you shouldn't go to the hospital? You look really pale.'

I hesitated for a moment. But far too many people already knew my secret. And Steve seemed to think I'd be all right. Whatever he was, whoever he worked for, he sounded like he knew what he was talking about. 'I'm OK,' I said, pulling off the sticky pads that held wires to my skin. The machine in the corner made a soft whining sound. 'I mean, I will be. I'm not dead, am I? So that's a start!'

Imogen looked at me and her lower lip wobbled. 'I thought you *might* be dead. Downstairs. It was **AWFUL**!'

We had a bit of a shaky hug. 'Come on,' I said. 'Let's find Joe.'

Steve had disappeared, and the paramedics were packing up their kit, shaking their heads and muttering about 'authorities'. The woman gave me a worried smile. 'Listen,' she said, 'if you feel at all woozy, get yourself down to A and E, all right? Your vital signs are all fine, but there may be effects that haven't yet appeared.'

I nodded. 'Thank you.'

Joe was standing by the railings, patting Thor, the huge black dog.

'There really IS a dog!' I exclaimed, relieved.

'Of course there's a dog,' Joe said. 'You been imagining things?'

I shook my head. 'I have no idea. Who is Steve the dog-walker really?'

'Head of a *shadowy government agency*,' he

said in delight. 'Isn't that just the **BEST**?'

I gave a snort. 'You're joking.'

'I'm so not.' He beamed. My brother was clearly in seventh heaven. 'I'm living my own comic strip. This is **the most awesome** day of my life.'

'*I nearly died*,' I pointed out.

He looked guilty for a moment. 'Yeah. Well, yeah, I suppose. Probably. But hey—I saved you!' He grinned again.

'Did you?'

'He did, actually,' Imogen added. 'He pushed the lever to switch off the Machine.'

'Oh,' I said. 'Oh—well, thanks. So I guess we all saved each other. I saved Imogen. Joe saved me.'

'And I saved us by stamping on the professor's foot,' Imogen said with satisfaction. 'We all did our bit.'

I looked around. In front of us, the huge CyberSky building still stood, but many of the windows had cracked, and smoke still oozed from various crevices. Three large black trucks had drawn up on the road, with tinted windows and no markings of any kind. They certainly looked like sinister government vehicles. There were two police cars, but the police themselves were in discussion with the people from the trucks, who were all dressed in full-body hazard suits. It was the weirdest scene I'd ever witnessed. 'Shouldn't we tell someone what happened?' I asked.

'I have,' Joe said. 'I told Steve everything. He's going to handle it all—the police won't come asking questions. His department sent him down here to investigate CyberSky and he's mad with himself for not realizing what was going on. He's totally cool about your powers.'

I stared at him. 'I thought you said we shouldn't tell people about my powers because they'd want to dissect my brain.'

'Well, yeah—but not *these* people. These people know *all* about stuff like that. Alien landings and supernatural events and stuff. They're like the only people in the country who actually KNOW it's all true. Steve pretends to be this crazy nut so that he can investigate things. He guessed you had powers when we met him earlier. I bet he's met loads of people like you.'

I felt slightly hurt.

Imogen took my arm. 'No one's like you,' she

said comfortingly. 'You're amazing.'

'Aw, thanks.'

Two cars came down the hill. At the wheel of the first, I could see my mum, pale and anxious. In the second—Imogen's parents, who jumped out of the car almost before it had stopped moving and dived on her, sobbing.

My mum stepped out of the car and winced. The migraine hadn't quite gone yet then. 'You two are in such trouble!' she said shakily. 'How could you go off by yourselves like that?' Then she caught sight of the busted CyberSky building and her jaw dropped. 'What on earth has been going on?'

Joe and I looked at each other. 'Are you going to tell her, or am I?' he asked.

'Tell her what?' I replied innocently.

He grinned. 'Your training is complete.'

CHAPTER 23

You know in films, after the big fight with the baddies, there's always the bit at the end where they tidy everything up? Well, this is that bit.

Mum drove me and Joe home. She made us hot drinks and insisted that we sit on the sofa and rest. Every now and then she held my face in her hands and went all wobbly over the burn pattern—which, by the way, was still up the sides of my cheeks and across my forehead, even though my powers (if I still had them) weren't switched on. After an hour, though, the marks on my cheek had faded completely. Only the twisting pink lines on my forehead remained.

Half an hour after we got back, Imogen's mum phoned and asked if they could come round with a takeaway. Her parents wanted to thank me and Joe for finding Imogen. I panicked for a bit that she'd told them everything, but I needn't have worried. Her parents were obviously under the impression she'd been accidentally locked in a store room and that Joe and I had made the professor search the building for her. Her mum even kissed me, which was a bit embarrassing. I saw Joe wiping his cheek after she kissed him too.

The CyberSky building was on the local news that evening, and they said there had been a **GAS EXPLOSION.** Joe, Imogen and I looked at each other. How many people knew the truth? A body had been found in the basement that unconfirmed reports suggested was Professor Macavity. I gulped at this. Imogen said, 'Good riddance,' and Joe said grimly under his breath, 'It won't be her. You'll see. Like Blofeld in James Bond. He always comes back. *She's your evil nemesis.*'

All the CyberSky phones stopped working. I was relieved that no one else would have their brains altered by the jellyfish worm-thing, but it was a bit of a pain to go back to my old phone and have no signal again. And Joe complained loudly that he desperately *needed* Mum to buy him one now.

We had pizza but I was dying to talk to the others so, as soon as we could, we escaped upstairs. 'Thank goodness,' Joe said, as we flopped onto my bed. 'I've got parent overload.'

I rubbed my head. 'This itches.'

Imogen said, 'It's healing. Nerve endings itch when they grow.' She blushed as I looked at her. 'What? It was on one of my quizzes. Don't look at me like that. I'm fine again now. It was just ... nice ... to feel special for a while ... '

'You ARE special,' I said. 'You're my best friend.'

Joe made puking noises. 'When you've quite finished,' he said, 'we have to talk about *that*.' He pointed at my head. 'You'll need a mask.'

'What? A mask? Why?'

He shrugged. 'If you're going to be a superhero, you're going to have to cover it up. Otherwise everyone'll know who you are. You'll need a costume too.'

'I am NOT wandering around in a pair of tights,' I told him firmly. 'Besides, I don't even know if I still *have* powers.'

'Course you do,' he said. 'They'll probably just take a few days to come back. You need a name too. As a superhero.'

'*Shockwave!*' cried Imogen, making me jump. 'Because, you know—electricity!'

'Er,' I said. 'I dunno. It doesn't feel very . . . *me*.' Her face fell. 'But it's a good suggestion,' I added hurriedly.

'You haven't told me how you got your powers,' she said. 'I've missed so much!'

There was a sudden faint but insistent beeping. Joe looked astonished. 'It's my phone!'

He reached into his back pocket and pulled out his CyberSky. We stared at it in disbelief. 'But they all stopped working,' I said. 'How come it's beeping?'

'I don't know.' Joe shook his head. 'It was dead as a dodo last time I looked. But somehow I've got a text message.'

He pressed his finger to the screen and it sprang into life. We all bent over it to read the words.

I KNOW WHO YOU ARE AND WHAT YOU ARE.

I DON'T FORGET MY ENEMIES.

ONE DAY, YOU AND I WILL MEET AGAIN, ELECTRIC GIRL

You could have heard a pin drop. I felt cold all over.

'Is it from . . . ' Imogen whispered. '*Her*?'

I took a breath. 'Who else could it be?'

'Who else could remote-activate my phone?' added Joe. His voice sounded quiet and unconfident. He looked at me. 'She's still alive. And she'll come after you.'

I felt a sudden anger sweep through me. 'Yeah? Well, she's not going to freak me out any more. We've beaten her once, we can do it again. I'm Electric Girl, remember?'

'**ELECTRIGIRL**?' said Imogen thoughtfully.

I nodded, clenching my fists. 'My new name. It's perfect.'

'But are you still electric?' she asked. 'I mean, do you still have your powers?'

'Let's find out,' I said, pointing at Joe's phone. 'Starting with THAT.'

Quickly, he put it on the floor before shuffling backwards. 'Don't get carried away,' he warned.

I smiled tightly. 'I know what I'm doing.' I took a breath and stretched out my hands . . .

ACKNOWLEDGEMENTS

This book has been through more developments than I can remember, and so many people have helped it on its way. Firstly, thanks to David and Ralph at Southern Electric, who were so kind and helpful when I wanted to know about electricity substations. David actually drove me to some of their stations to show me the busbars and explain the dangers of an electrical arc. After talking to them, I decided not to set Holly's transformation in a substation!

Thanks to my amazing writer friends, who have given thoughtful and valuable feedback on various drafts: Liz Kessler, Lee Weatherly and Susie Day. Also to Steve Cole, who not only read the opening chapters more than once but also lent me his precious Spider-Man comics and gave me the great advice: 'Just blow everything up.'

Thanks to Penny Holroyde, who was so patient through the many pre-submission stages of this book. And to the team at OUP, particularly Kathy Webb, Gill Sore and Holly Fulbrook who have made the whole process such a joy—and I really mean that.

Thanks to my husband Phil for unfailing support throughout the 'journey', and to our kids Jemima and Harriet, who deserve a wider range of female superheroes to dress up as.

Finally, the biggest thanks to Cathy Brett, who signed up well before this project ever came under an editor's critical eye, and who has shared all the highs and lows and consistently produced incredible work that makes my jaw drop. Thanks, partner!

ABOUT THE AUTHOR

Jo Cotterill believes that superheroes are really important. They are what we can all aspire to be: people who use their powers to fight evil and help others. When she's not trying to change the world, Jo makes up stories in her very untidy office-come-craft room, sometimes stopping to write music instead. Her other books include the *Sweet Hearts* series for Random House and the critically-acclaimed *Looking at the Stars*, which was nominated for the Carnegie Medal. Jo lives in Oxfordshire with her husband, daughters and two over-indulged guinea pigs.

www.jocotterill.com

ABOUT THE ILLUSTRATOR

Cathy Brett has been a theatre scenic artist, school art technician, college lecturer, fashion illustrator, packaging designer, jet-setting spotter of global trends and style consultant to the British high street. These days she loves drawing more than anything else. Ever. Except her nieces. And cake. Drawing her nieces while eating cake would be utter bliss.

Cathy lives and works in a shed/ studio at the bottom of a Surrey garden.

www.cathybrett.blogspot.co.uk

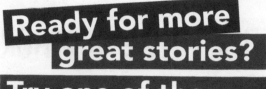

Ready for more great stories? Try one of these...

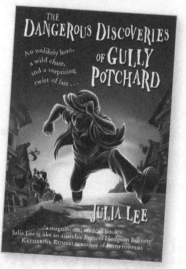

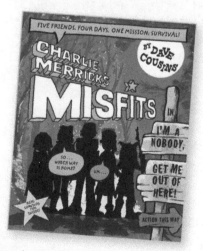

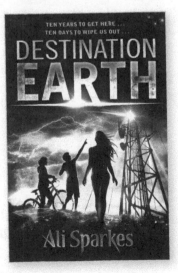